I0731384

GANG RUMBLE

EDWARD S. AARONS
WRITING AS
EDWARD RONNS

Black Gat Books • Eureka California

GANG RUMBLE

Published by Black Gat Books
A division of Stark House Press
1315 H Street
Eureka, CA 95501, USA
griffinskye3@sbcglobal.net
www.starkhousepress.com

GANG RUMBLE
Originally published by Avon Publications, Inc., New York, as by Edward Ronns, and copyright © 1958 by Edward Ronns.

Copyright © 2021 by Stark House Press. All rights reserved under International and Pan-American Copyright Conventions.

ISBN-13: 978-1-951473-53-2

Cover and text design by Jeff Vorzimmer, ¡caliente!design, Austin, Texas
Proofreading by Bill Kelly
Cover art from the film poster for *Sindacato del Porto*

PUBLISHER'S NOTE:
This is a work of fiction. Names, characters, places and incidents are either the products of the author's imagination or used fictionally, and any resemblance to actual persons, living or dead, events or locales, is entirely coincidental.

Without limiting the rights under copyright reserved above, no part of this publication may be reproduced, stored, or introduced into a retrieval system or transmitted in any form or by any means (electronic, mechanical, photocopying, recording or otherwise) without the prior written permission of both the copyright owner and the above publisher of the book.

First Stark House Press/Black Gat Edition: December 2021

"... a masterful storyteller."
—*Paperback Warrior*
"... his prose was propulsive and machine tooled and this is an absorbing quick read for devotees of the pacy thriller."
—F. J. Harvey

"The city streets became a jungle of fear and terror!"
—original cover blurb

"... Aarons manages to sustain the fast pace right up to the final paragraph."
—John Pringle

Chapter One

Pete came over to where Johnny Broom lay sprawled on the roof coping and said, "Listen, kid, what are you trying to prove?"

Johnny didn't turn his head. "Go away, Petey-O."

"Get down off there," Pete said. "You want to kill yourself, is that it?"

"You'll be late for work," Johnny said.

"Come on, get down!"

"Ah, shut up."

Pete's heavy working shoes made crunching noises on the tar-and-gravel flat roof. He stood beside Johnny, his big hands opening and closing with tension, and looked down at the street. "What are you watching?"

"Nothing. The street. Everything"

"You know something, kid? You're crazy. Crazy with the heat."

"It's hot, all right."

"Just be careful, will you?" Pete asked. The begging, whining note was in his voice. He could never keep up the big-brother act for long. *The yuk*, Johnny thought. He felt a tide of anger in him, and then he began to laugh, making quick, barking sounds against the pressure of the evening heat. Pete looked disconcerted. "So what's so funny?"

Johnny didn't answer. He didn't know why he was laughing, because there actually was nothing funny; and admitting it to himself, he felt a twist of fear in his belly, deep down, like something hot wriggling in his gut. He pretended Pete wasn't there. He *willed* Big Pete to go away. Not for the first time, he wished something would happen to Pete so he wouldn't keep dragging at him all the time, every minute of the day.

They were brothers, but they didn't look alike. Where Johnny was tall and thin and wiry for his age, with thick blond hair kept in a careful wave with pomatum, with gray eyes too wise for his seventeen years, Pete, near thirty, was big and lumpy like an ox, Johnny thought. And he wondered what an ox really looked like. He'd never seen such an animal. Maybe they'd all died out by now, or something. You never heard of anybody with an ox. But that's what Pete was, anyway. A living, human-type ox.

It was three years now since the old man died, and Pete took over running the house for just the two of them. There wasn't much difference, Johnny thought, between Pete and the old man.

He kept watching the street. Stitch Pollard ought to be along soon. Where in hell was the dumb, scared bastard?

"What time is it?" he asked Pete.

"Soon be eight."

"What *time?*"

"Ten to. You goin' on the air, or something, you got know the split second?"

"Thanks for nothing," Johnny said.

"Johnny?"

Johnny was silent.

"Get down off there, Johnny."

It wasn't worth answering. Pete wouldn't go away. The jerk would be late for his watchman's job. A big deal, that was. But it was all Pete knew, all he would ever know, and even if it paid for the groceries for the two of them, it wasn't good enough for Johnny Broom. Johnny Broom had decided to go places. And tonight he was going to take the first step.

The evening sky looked explosive over Philadelphia's dim, dreary reaches, seen from the rooftop of the brick row house on North Seventh. The Jungle, they called it in the newspaper stories and the editorials in the *Bulletin* and the *Inquirer*. Johnny read the stories and laughed, and sometimes he felt sick about it, all those do-gooders and social workers wondering what to do about the people and conditions in the Jungle. But it was just the old neighborhood, Johnny thought, nothing bad or good about it. It was just something that had always been here and always would. He didn't want to change any of it. It was home.

He lay on the coping of the roof edge and sweated. Pete lit a cigarette and shuffled his feet in his heavy work shoes and looked as if he wanted to talk some more. He didn't offer Johnny a butt. To hell with the dumb ox. He had his own. But he didn't want to smoke right now.

Where in Jesus was Stitch?

It was going to be one of those nights when the streets melted and the walls fell in. One of those stinking hot nights where every crappy smell of every crappy person in the city would be strong enough to walk on. There was no breeze, even up here on the roof. There were towering clouds in the sky to the east, over the Delaware, and the tops of the clouds were red. Johnny tried to imagine the mushroom of an A-bomb, but he wasn't interested enough to follow it out. He didn't see anything to get wet in the pants about over the bomb. It was a fact of life, something that had always been there, like the dirty street and the old house under the roof below him and the dirty pink-white rose wallpaper in his back room.

He leaned farther over the coping, because he wanted to see the sidewalk a little better and because he knew it would bother Pete. Old Mrs. Kramer was sitting on the steps two houses down, fanning herself with a rag. From up here, you could practically see right down her dress. Some snotty kids were playing over near Feeney's candy store on the corner—probably figuring how to get over the wooden fence into the backyard and snatch a free bottle of Coke from the cases usually stacked there. They'd be disappointed. From the roof, Johnny could see that old Feeney had finally caught on and removed the Coke cases into the back room behind the store. He laughed about it, looking at the dumb squirts down there, figuring out how to swipe a handful of nothing.

"Johnny, listen," Pete said.

"What time is it now?"

"Never mind the time. Don't you want to come with me? I told Harrison you'd take the job."

"Tough titty for you, Petey-O."

"But it's a good job, Johnny."

"It stinks."

"And we could use the dough, Johnny."

"Ah, we're doing all right."

"Look, you said yourself you weren't going back to school in September. You said you'd get a job."

"I said I'd *think* about it," Johnny answered. "So I'm thinking."

Pete looked angry, and his big hands moved as if he wanted to yank Johnny down from the coping. He didn't do it. He was afraid to try anything, now. Not since this spring, when Johnny grew taller than Pete and had the knife ready. Johnny turned his head and looked at Pete with cool gray eyes. It was a look he had used before, deliberately, and he knew it scared his older brother. That time with the knife, that had been a boff. That time Johnny said he wasn't going back to that lousy school and Pete had tried to murder him, like he used to. The knife was the old equalizer, all right. Johnny still had it downstairs in the bedroom. Pete knew it was down there now, but he was scared of it, just the same. Pete licked his lips and said: "What are you going to do tonight?"

It was just a question.

"Nothing," Johnny said.

"So what's nothing? You going over to the Club?"

"What for?"

"It's a nice, decent place. Mr. Stephens is working hard at it. He wants all you Lancers to join, and he's the best friend you punks ever had, only you don't know it. It's a cool pad for you, Johnny. There's a dance scheduled for tonight, Saturday night. With live music."

Johnny laughed. "It's for crums."

"There's nothing the matter with the Neighborhood Club, Johnny. The matter is with you, and those Lancers. You'll get in trouble with the Lancers."

"It's my club," Johnny said proudly.

"Because they gave you that stupid title? They elected you warlord?" Pete blew out his breath. "For god's sake, what kind of stupidity is that?"

Johnny said nothing.

"You're just a dumb kid playing with fire," Pete said. "You'll wind up in jail or get killed."

"You're dragging me, Petey-O. Lay off, huh?"

"I don't know what to do with you," Pete sighed.

"So do nothing."

"You've got something on for tonight?"

Again! But it was just a question, even the second time. Johnny felt the squirt of worry in him, and he looked at Pete. But Pete couldn't know anything about it. Pete didn't know anything but eating, sleeping, and working his ass off at that crummy warehouse watchman's job. Pete didn't even have a girl. What was Pete's life good for, anyway?

"I swear to God, kid, I think you're nuts," Pete said. He was still remembering that time with the knife. He licked his lips. "All right, kid, I'm shoving. You need any money?"

"No."

"I could give you a couple bucks."

"Not enough," Johnny said.

"Not enough for *what*, for Chrissake?"

"I don't know," Johnny said.

"Listen, kid, what eats you? What do you *want*?"

Johnny gave him the cool look. "I want to cut your goddam stupid throat, you jerk. Will you stop dragging me?"

Pete said: "Hell, I give up. I'm going."

"Good riddance."

"Take it easy, you hear? See you later."

You sure will, Johnny thought. But he didn't say it, and Pete went away.

Good thing. Stitch Pollard came around the corner just then and headed for the house.

Stitch was fat and stubby, with a saddle nose and thin red hair and blue eyes so pale they made you think he had to be blind. He always smelled. There was something about Stitch's sweat, maybe from something he always ate, that made him smell different from other people. And when Johnny thought about it, he hated the idea of having to stick close to Pollard tonight, of all nights, when it was so hot. Maybe he could take Stitch for a quick dive in the river. But he knew Stitch wouldn't do it. Stitch hated water. He could swim, but he was afraid of it.

Rose Vallera came out of her house on the corner opposite Feeney's, and Stitch bumped into her. Blind. Johnny laughed. He wouldn't mind bumping into a piece like old Rose, and maybe Stitch wasn't so dumb at that, grabbing a quick feel of her through that thin cotton dress. From the roof coping, Johnny could see Rose saying something to Stitch, and Stitch smiled with his big, fat moon face and bent backward and then bowed to her in an exaggerated gesture to let her go by, and that only made Rose get madder. When she walked away on her high heels, her flesh bounded and it was something to see, the way she walked.

Johnny wished that Flopsy, for Chrissake, could get to look even a little bit like Rose.

Rose wasn't afraid of Stitch or any of the Lancers because of her old man, Sergeant Thomas Vallera. In Johnny's book, Vallera was an old grafter, and he knew for a fact that the sergeant was a secret boozer. But he was tough, and Johnny respected toughness. He remembered the old man once talking to Lew McGee, who was Vallera's partner in the prowlie, telling him about the Lancers.

"They act like animals, you got to treat 'em like animals," Vallera had snarled. "Tame 'em with your fists, a club, a whip. That's the only things the punks understand."

A lot that old son of a bitch knew. Someday, Johnny thought, he'd fix things to show Vallera what the score really was. But not tonight. Someday, but not now. He felt a good warmth in him when he thought about it.

Lew McGee wasn't too bad. He went around with Rose, and it looked like Lew might marry Rose, if Vallera ever decided anybody was good enough to marry her. Lew's chances didn't look too bright, but he was persistent. He took a lot of abuse from the sergeant, just to stay in good and be able to take Rose out to a movie, or to Fairmount Park for a quick grab on a hot night like this.

Johnny wished he could step into Lew's shoes for

just a few minutes, out in the park with Rose.

But all cops were crums, anyway. Who'd want to be cop?

Stitch was still standing down there, leaning against the wire fence, watching Rose walk away. Johnny felt irritated. Didn't the smelly jerk know they had serious business tonight? But Stitch just watched the way Rose walked in her cotton dress.

The hairpin fence that Stitch leaned on went all the way around the corner. The Vallera house, being a corner house and not in the middle of the row, was the biggest, and it was detached from the others, which made it something special. It looked better than all the others, too. But why not? Johnny thought. The old bastard shook down enough in graft to live it up plenty.

Finally Stitch came across the street and walked into Johnny's house, which was never locked, and yelled for Johnny. Johnny perversely didn't answer. Let Stitch find him. But Stitch kept yelling his name, and Johnny couldn't stand it after a minute and went to the roof hatch and called to Stitch down the ladder.

Stitch came up, and he brought his smell with him. He wore dungarees and the solid dark red singlet that was the uniform of the Lancers. You knew a Lancer in the summer by their red tee-shirts, just like you knew a member of the Violets by that stupid purple silk shirt they liked to show around.

"What took you so long?" Johnny asked.

"I ain't late, am I?"

"I've been waiting."

"It ain't even dark yet, Johnny."

That was Stitch all over, a fat smelly slob. Whiny, just like Pete. "Where are all the guys?" Johnny asked.

"They'll be ready. Ten sharp, like you said. It's your operation, Johnny. A lot of guys don't understand it, though. I think you're taking a big chance."

"The Violets go bowling tonight, don't they?"

Stitch nodded. "At Sandor's, like always."

"So we attack them there."

"But the orders you give don't make sense. You call for a rumble, okay, we're with you. But on a night like this, the cops got a worried look, you know? And somebody said there was a spill. Somebody said the Violets know, and they'll be waiting for us, Johnny. They'll murder us, if the cops don't lid the steamer first. What kind of an operation is it, they ask?"

Johnny grinned. "You and me won't be there long, Stitch."

Stitch rubbed his saddle nose, spit on the roof, and stuck his hands in his denim pockets. He smelled worse than ever. "I know, but it's an awful chance, Johnny. I know we got another operation, just you and me, but deserting the guys in a rumble just to pull off something else—"

"The rumble will cover us."

"It kills me, Johnny. Your own brother!"

"So what? You got brothers, haven't you?"

"Yeah, but Pete—he never done any harm—"

Johnny pretended anger. He didn't want Stitch to chicken out now. Stitch had the wheels, and they needed wheels tonight. Without warning, he grabbed Stitch by his sweaty red shirt and yanked him forward, then jabbed a stiff thumb into Stitch's throat at just the right place. Stitch started to yelp, and the yelp became a strangled cough, and he twisted away and fell to his knees on the hot, soft tar and gravel of the roof. His face turned purple and his eyes popped and stared at Johnny in agony and disbelief.

"Get up," Johnny said.

"Oh, you bastard—" Stitch moaned.

"You're not hurt. Get up. That was just a lesson. Only the beginning. You got to learn discipline, you crum. You got to learn to take orders and do what you're told, what I tell you, never mind those jerks in the Lancers! And you don't ask any goddam fool questions, you understand?"

"Yeah, Johnny...."

"Get up."

Stitch stood up. There was a dark thumbprint on his neck that would stay there for a day or two and remind him who and what Johnny Broom was. Stitch didn't understand, but he didn't have to. Stitch still clung to kid loyalties, worrying about the Lancers. But Johnny knew better now. He felt far superior to Stitch, keeping his knowledge to himself. Loyalty never bought a man a damned thing. It was dog eat dog, and when you had a chance to go up, to do something big, you took it, and to hell with the others. They'd sell you out just as fast, no matter how loyal you were to the gang. Johnny looked at Stitch for a moment and then turned away, fishing in his pocket for a crumpled pack of Camels. He lit one and watched Stitch relax a little, but Stitch wouldn't meet his eyes.

"So tell me about Comber," Johnny said.

"Comber says it's up to you," Stitch whispered.

"Is Comber scared too?"

"Not him. You know Comber, Johnny. You want to work for him, it's up to you, he says. Get in the warehouse. You're the only one who can do it. It's your own brother who's watchman, after all. If Pete gets hurt—"

"Nobody gets hurt."

"Well, all right," Stitch said. He rubbed his saddle nose again. "But if the rest of the Lancers knew you were goin' to pull out of the rumble while the cops maybe play Jesus-Mary with the guys, it won't be good."

"Who's to know? You and me and Comber."

"That's right, Johnny."

"And Mike."

Stitch's pale, blind-blue eyes went round. "Him?"

"Him. Mike."

"He's a creep."

"He's tough," Johnny said.

"He makes things seem so queer, always."

"You'll be with me. Mike's all right."

"He scares me, that's all," Johnny said. "A creep."

"We need one more hand. We can't trust a Lancer. He's a loner, right? So he doesn't spill it to the guys, and the guys never know, and then you and me, we go up the ladder and work for Comber. We'll cut Mike in. Comber says there's a hundred a piece for each of us when the truck is loaded."

Stitch held out a fat, grimy hand and said feebly: "Johnny, you don't know nothing about Mike. Not even his last name. Or where he lives or comes from. He talks different, he—"

"I know," Johnny said. "He's a creep. Maybe we can use a creep tonight."

Chapter Two

At eight-fifteen of that Saturday night, Mike Tarrant lay on his back in bed and waited for dark to come. There was an impatience in him that silently screamed for the sun to hurry in its cycle and go down in the west, bringing the hot, stilly night. He lay still and waited. His finely chiseled face was immobile, his smoothly carved lips quiet except for a very faint quivering at the corners of his mouth that no one would ever notice. He was handsome in a way that allowed him to acknowledge his good looks as just one more thing he had which was due him.

His room was quiet and peaceful. The Tarrant house, in the new Society Hill section downtown, just off Locust Street, was like an island floating with moats and castellated walls in defense against the slum-clearance projects and ancient buildings being torn down in dust and rubble for the new Mall around Independence Hall. Big deal, Mike thought lazily. He considered the house and the neighborhood without rancor. He felt that moving here was an idle gesture, following the Mayor and others from Darby and the Main Line, back into the heart of the city that had been abandoned for several generations because of the tide of color and the poor who had darkened it.

He had liked it better out in the suburbs, in the old house. But this place had its advantages. It was close to his favorite scenes of action. And easy to return to.

Why didn't the sun go down?

He had the feeling sometimes that if he willed hard enough and long enough, he could make time stand still for him or speed up, whichever was more convenient at the moment. Or he could make himself invisible. It was a game he had played since childhood, and at seventeen, he still used it to lull himself to sleep, when sleep was hard to reach. He used it as a barrier against those other dreams that made him sweat and tremble with unnamed fears.

He could control the world and all the poor, ugly, ignorant slobs in it, if he could only learn the secret. He had to concentrate on it, think about it some more. It would come to him. He was sure of it.

Otherwise, the thought of living out his life according to the stupid, boring rules that governed everybody else was an agony and a black torment he could not endure.

His room was quiet and cool. The air-conditioner made a barrier against the heat of evening, humming discreetly, the streamers like wild thin fingers fluttering in the air above the fans. It was a fine room, fresh and new, furnished with Colonial antiques that Mother had hunted for in Bucks County and out in Lancaster. She was so eager to please, Mike thought, she was pitiful. He didn't exactly hate her. He simply held her in contempt.

The sycamore tree in the back garden made dappled shadows on the green and white wallpaper. But the light had a red quality in it, and Mike began to shiver.

He told himself he shouldn't go out tonight.

Not tonight. He had promised himself he wouldn't go again.

Downstairs, he heard the genteel murmur of conversation as his father and mother finished dinner with their guest, Henry Dexter Stephens.

This Henry Dexter Stephens was a real bug, Mike thought. His mind turned into a cauldron of bitter acid. The dirty, hypocritical bastard was hipped about kids. On the Governor's Committee for Investigating Juvenile Delinquency. An old-time Philadelphian, member of the Assembly, even, but he didn't know which end was up. He was always spouting off about understanding youth and helping them to find themselves in a world of chaotic confusion.

Don't go out tonight!

The words came in small acid bubbles through the

seething mass of his thoughts. He rolled on the bed and groaned and sweated. He sat up and let his bare feet dangle over the edge of the bed and hunched over as if he had a belly cramp. He needed a drink. But the bottle he'd hidden in the closet was empty. The old man would have a purple fit if he knew about the drinking. *And* the other things. But nobody knew. Nobody would ever know. He'd be safe if he quit tonight, if he didn't go out.

But he knew he was going to meet Johnny Broom.

"Michael?"

His mother's voice whispered with soft anxiety up the gleaming, polished stairs, slid along the white-painted banister rail, came down the wide bedroom hall and through the closed door, and closed around his ears to explode in a violent blossom of hatred. Why didn't she leave him alone?

"Michael, can you come down for a moment?"

He didn't reply.

He stood up and saw himself in the mirror. He was not large for his age. At seventeen, he had the looks of a boy two or three years younger. He had a baby face, under thick, wavy black hair. Women loved to touch him, seemed unable to resist running their fingers through his hair, exclaiming over his looks. Some women went much farther. He remembered when they lived out at Crestwood, the big house on the Main Line. He'd been just twelve when Mrs. Connover did that thing to him. She'd been a neighbor, a little blond woman with a tiny waist and remarkable hips and bust. His parents had been at the country club, and he'd been alone in his bedroom. He hadn't heard her come into the house. He didn't even know she was there until she stood in the doorway and caught him at it. She had flushed and then her eyes went all wide and funny and then she laughed and came to the bed and sat beside him and her voice was different, somehow, telling him he shouldn't do that, it was such a terrible waste. And then she showed him what he should do....

He thought of Irene Connover with a spurt of terrible hatred that shook him until he had to sit down again. The shame, the humiliation, and then the hunger of her, the way she *absorbed* him, laughing all the time, with the queerness in her voice....

But he'd fixed her good. Mike laughed softly as his angry memory ebbed. Caught her with that fat Frank Olland, from down the road, that afternoon a couple weeks later. The look on their faces! He felt gleeful, remembering. He'd shaken down Olland for over eight hundred dollars before the Connovers suddenly moved away.

And there were other women after that. He learned to use the way they fawned over his good looks. But you had to be careful not to make a mistake. Some would, some wouldn't. Some were shocked, some wept and struck themselves afterward, feeling guilt for what they had done with a boy.

Mike didn't think of himself as a. boy. He felt old, old.

"Michael, aren't you well? Why didn't you answer your mother?"

His father stood there. Dr. Irving Tarrant, the Pine Street snob.

"Michael?"

"I—I was asleep, Dad," he whispered.

"We want you to say goodnight to Mr. and Mrs. Stephens."

"All right, Dad. Fine."

"He's interested in young people, you know."

"Yes."

A flicker of passing concern in the iron-gray face,

the cool eyes, distrusting but not really seeing his son's illness. Like the cobbler's kids who run around without shoes, Mike thought. The old man was a doctor, but he never bothered to take care of his own family, never saw what was right under his long patrician nose.

And a good thing, a good thing, Mike thought fervently.

Dr. Tarrant looked at Mike and never saw his own son.

Mike, dressed in a gray sharkskin suit and a white shirt and sober bowtie, went downstairs into the gracious drawing room and met the Stephens, Henry Dexter Stephens and his wife, Louise. Louise smiled warmly and shook hands and presently ran her fingers through his wavy hair. Mike looked at her and she flushed and when he kept looking at her, she moved away.

He knew all about Stephens. Henry Dexter's handsome, blond head was pictured almost daily in the *Inquirer* or the *Bulletin*. The best friend of youth in the city, the headlines read. Setting up neighborhood youth clubs, inviting whole gangs to join, organizing dances and games with free refreshments, all that crap, Mike thought. But some of the fighting gangs had actually been dissolved through Stephens' efforts. Maybe they were just playing it cool while Stephens' heat was on; but they had broken up, nevertheless. Everybody was talking admiringly about how Stephens understood young people so well.

It was enough to make you vomit, Mike thought.

"Well, Michael," Stephens said, with that hearty joviality that made him a good politician—he was going to run for Mayor, or Governor, next election—"If all the youngsters were like you, I'd probably be out of a job, don't you think?"

"I couldn't say, sir," Mike replied. "I don't think I—I'm not such a paragon of virtue."

There was polite adult laughter, condescending to him. He didn't miss the way his mother looked at his father. His mother knew why he'd been kicked out of Penn Academy. Nobody else knew, and nobody ever would. She was afraid to talk.

"You know the sort of work I'm doing, don't you, Mike?" Stephens said. He held a brandy glass in his slim, elegant hand, and Mike felt a dryness in his throat. He needed a drink badly. "I'd like to talk to you about it some time. Get the views of someone in your age group, you know, outside of the Jungle, see what you think of the problem."

"Yes, sir. That would be interesting, sir. But I don't think I would be of much help. I don't know very much about it."

"Your parents think you are a brilliant young man."

"Too brilliant, perhaps," Dr. Tarrant put in. He waved a deprecating hand. "Parents are apt to be prejudiced about the virtues of their own youngsters."

"Yes, that is one facet of the situation we continually encounter," Stephens said. "This is a generation adrift and footloose in a world of confusion and hatred, cold war, atomic bombs, space adventure, television—a situation such as society has never really met before. The old disciplines and isolations have broken down. You can't blame the youngsters when the adults are even more confused and filled with tensions than they. Parental discipline cannot compete with the psycho-persuaders of politics and commerce today. The authority and disciplinary image of the father no longer exists. Don't blame the boys for running wild in a crazy world. They're trying to find stability in their own organizations and creeds—and unfortunately, gang organizations seem the easiest answer. We hope to overcome that, but it is not a simple task."

Louise Stephens looked quickly at Mike again, a question in her eyes, and as quickly looked away when he returned her stare.

"I dare say," Stephens said, turning to Mike, "you could be quite a bit of help to me, young man. The viewpoint of youth, you know." Mike looked at him with bland eyes, noting the fact that Stephens used pomade to keep his blond hair groomed, and had neutral nail polish on his fingernails. Stephens' shaving lotion had a tweedy scent. His voice rolled on, too friendly, too adult, too man-to-man. "You know, Mike, I have an idea. I'm visiting one of my Neighborhood Youth Clubs tonight. Just recently set it up. The one on North Seventh. I'm going there tonight. How would you like to come along with me, Mike?"

His mother made a small sound of protest. "I don't think Michael—"

"Why not?" his father said, voice booming. "Might be good for the boy. See the problems other youngsters have to face. Might make him appreciate a good home, education, and all that."

Stephens looked annoyed. "I simply thought that Mike might have some useful suggestions, that's all." He looked at Mike. "What do you say? Unless you have a date tonight, young fellow—"

"I'd rather not," Mike said. "I don't care to see that sort of thing."

Stephens laughed. "Squeamish, boy?"

"Maybe, sir. I've only driven through the Jungle once. I didn't like it."

"But it's there. You can't close your eyes to facts."

"I—I'd rather not," Mike said. "I don't—it's too different from what I'm used to...."

His mother murmured: "Michael has always been so sheltered, Mr. Stephens."

"Well, all right. It was just a sudden idea," Stephens said, yielding.

"I'm sorry, Mr. Stephens," Mike said.

"Perfectly all right, son."

Mike turned to his parents. "May I be excused, please?"

"Of course, Michael."

He wanted to run, to yell and curse and spit at their stupid faces. But he made himself shake hands with his father's guests and went back upstairs.

He used the servants' stairway in the rear of the big brick house. On the way, he passed the library and lifted a bottle of Scotch from his father's bar. He needed it.

He sat on the edge of the bed and shook with chill, despite the heat of the evening. *Don't go out, don't go out,* the voices said. Stephens will be in the neighborhood. Somebody might see you, recognize you. The voices kept clamoring in his brain. He opened the bottle of liquor and drank deeply from it, breathed out, breathed in, drank again, and fell back on the bed. He had to go. It was something he couldn't resist. Uptown with Johnny Broom, or prowling about alone, that was the only reality. This room, his parents, the boredom and the waiting and the politeness and the goddam uselessness of it all— all this was nothing. You weren't alive here. You were only alive in the dark, moving on silent feet, looking and watching and doing things nobody knew about, except those to whom the doing of it was done. And they never knew. Nobody knew who he was. He'd been smart, careful. All it took was a little brains, and you could live like a king, like a god, above the laws that ruled everybody else. You could pull the strings and watch the puppets jump and dance in pain, sometimes crying, sometimes dying. The feeling he got from such night expeditions was like nothing else in the world.

The world was a stupid place, anyway. Anybody with a little brains and guts could run it.

It was eight-forty when Mike Tarrant got up. He looked and acted differently from the way he had been a few minutes ago.

John Dexter Stephens and Louise had left. His parents had gone out for the Saturday night bridge game with the Evansons.

He changed his clothes once more. He had the other outfit hidden in Jane's room, where no one could find it and suspect. Jane Quarles lived in the servants' quarters, on the third floor of the house, toward the rear. She was thirty, and she served as cook and maid for the Tarrants. She was short and inclined to plumpness, with a round, placid face and babyish blue eyes too often tearful. Mike always referred to her as Miss Quarles when anyone might overhear. It was easy enough to control Jane. He gave her what she needed, a kind of hopeless, tormenting, fearful love that had come from her first, uncertain, timid advances toward him last year. She loved him and feared him now. Once in a while, she told him, she thought of killing herself, because of the futility of her life, of the hopelessness of her situation. He was seventeen, she was thirty. She was only a cook and maid. She had no family, no one in the world. Only Mike, she told him.

Jane was in her room when he went up to her for his clothes. She had a small, portable television set, the audio turned down low, and she jumped up and snapped it off when he closed the door behind him.

"Oh, Michael...."

"I'm going out tonight," he said.

"Oh. I thought you—I thought we—your folks being away this evening—"

"I've got other business."

She trembled when he patted her shoulder. She had some tropical fish in a tank near the window, and he went over to them, expecting her to fetch his denims and cheap chambray shirt while he looked at them. But she didn't move. "Do you have to go out?" she whispered. "Do you, dear?"

"Get my clothes," he said. "Come on, come *on!*"

"Of course, darling. But I wish—"

"You make me sick," he said. "You're nagging, you know?"

"I don't mean to—I mean, I only worry about you, dear, when you go out on these—these expeditions of yours. I mean, well, you get all different, like, and I don't understand you—"

"Will you *move?*" he shouted. He wanted to kill her. "God, you get me stacked off, sometimes."

"All right, Michael." Her soft mouth shook and trembled, grew wet. Her eyes filled with tears and she turned hurriedly and got the denim slacks and the shirt, the sneakers he had painted black. He looked at her rump as she bent over into the closet. He wanted to kick her, just once, good and hard. Send her head smashing through the wall. She came to him with the clothes then and said, not looking at him: "Don't stare at me like that, Michael."

"Why not?"

"I don't like—it's not like you at all. Sometimes you can be so sweet and kind—so *good*—and then, I mean, like now, I hardly know you."

"I'll try to be back early," he said.

Her face lit up as if he had promised her eternity.

He would have to get rid of Jane pretty soon, he decided.

Chapter Three

Patrolman Lew McGee watched Johnny Broom and Stitch Pollard walk up Seventh Street and turn the corner to the east. It was eight forty-five, Saturday night, and the city breathed like a slumbering beast, stirring restlessly in the electric heat that built up and built up and seemed ready to explode. The clouds had cut off the shattering sunlight, and shadows lay like dirty pools on the cracked sidewalks and gutters of the Jungle. It would soon be dark, and then the animal that lived here, the great, inchoate mass of humanity, would begin to stir, to hunt, to steal, to hurt, to wound and kill.

Like those two young punks he had just watched out of sight.

He felt a quickening in him, like the slowly built-up tempo of a drum beat. It wasn't just the summer night, though.

Vallera was late again, and that wasn't unusual, but Lew didn't know what to do about it. You could cover it just so long, you had to, because he was Rose's father; but it couldn't go on forever.

The old man's drinking was getting past the point where it could be controlled. It was as if something drove Vallera remorselessly and urgently toward self-destruction.

It wasn't as if the sergeant ever said thank you, or indicated in any way that something was wrong. Lew didn't expect any thanks. He just wanted Vallera to hate him a little less, to admit that it would be a good thing if he and Rose got married soon.

But the sergeant had reached the point where you couldn't even talk to him anymore. He knew it all. He was a cop from grizzled head to tired feet, and when he was a cop, he was the best there was in all of Philadelphia.

Nobody knew the Jungle better than Vallera.

And Lew knew he could learn a lot from the old man.

The trouble was, Vallera with his rough-and-tumble background, his law of the fist and discipline, had an innate suspicion of any cop with a college education. And Lew had only two more years of night school at Temple to get his law degree.

Lew had been born and raised on Seventh Street. It had been different, then, twenty-odd years ago. Quieter, cleaner, not the slum it was today. He didn't feel as if he recognized it anymore. Coming back from Korea had been a shock. New people had moved in; Porto Ricans and Negroes pressed hard against the noose that strangled them and kept them tied to dilapidated, depressed neighborhoods. You couldn't blame them for wanting something better. They were entitled to it, just as the earlier waves of new people had struggled for better things, the things America had to offer.

The only problem was what to do about them now, to help them adjust. And to help the kids.

Kids like Johnny Broom and Stitch Pollard— Vallera said you had to beat them, whip them, treat them like animals. Lew couldn't go along with that. Somewhere, there had to be a bridge of understanding. You had to reach them and help them somehow. But how? They were like strangers; they spoke a different language.

Lew had volunteered to help with the Henry Dexter Stephens Neighborhood Club. He had little enough time to spare, between the tours of duty in the patrol car, and his classes in law and economics. But he did what he could. He knew it wasn't enough, but he tried.

Rose tried, too. She served regularly as a hostess at the Club. Some of the punks and hoodlums showed signs of recognizing a new and different set of values from the values and the laws of the Jungle they lived in. The hard core of resistance was in the Lancers. They had come to the Club just once, and it had been like an invasion of storm troopers. Dread and terror stalked into the place with them.

But nothing had happened that time.

They had looked, and eaten the refreshments, and even danced once or twice. And then they left quietly and never came back.

In a way, it was worse than if they had rioted and wrecked the place. Silence and scorn couldn't be handled. It wasn't tangible enough. It slid through your fingers like water, beyond your grasp.

There just wasn't any communication at all.

Lew looked at his watch again. Almost nine.

What was keeping Vallera? One last drink? Talking to Rose? He wished Rose would come out for just a minute or two.

He waited in the patrol car, watching Vallera's doorway.

When the door opened, it was Rose, after all. She came down the steps and opened the gate in the wire hairpin fence and crossed the sidewalk and came around the patrol car to the driver's side, where Lew waited. Her smile was tired.

"Hi. He'll be right out," she said.

"How is he?"

"He's all right, Lew."

"I've got to call Precinct soon. I can't wait."

Rose bit her lip. "He says not to call, Lew. He's already called, from the house." She paused. "He was talking to Comber, too."

"Comber? Again?"

"Please, Lew. He knows what he's doing."

"Comber's a hood, halfway up to the big time." Lew felt anger. "Why does he stay friends with Comber?"

"I don't know. And I just can't ask him. I don't even want to talk about it anymore."

Lew looked at her. He thought she was beautiful, and she was. He yearned and ached for her, and he dreamed of different and better things for the two of them. He liked everything about her—the way her dark hair fell softly to her shoulders, the way she walked, with pride and grace, her cleanliness, the crispness of her dress no matter what the heat might be. He grinned at her.

"Whatever you say, sweetheart."

"Lew—"

He saw the worry-shadow in her eyes. "What is it?"

"Be careful tonight," she said.

"I'm always careful, honey."

"But especially tonight. Take care of him, too."

"He wouldn't accept anything from me," Lew said. "Not advice or help or anything. You know that."

"But take care of him anyway. You can do it."

The worry-shadows were deeper now. "What's bothering you, Rose? It's just a routine tour of duty."

"I don't know. It's Saturday night and it's so hot and everything is so quiet. Too quiet. Do you know what I mean?"

"You're just nervous from the heat, honey. Take a cool bath, and you'll feel better." He grinned. "Think of me scrubbing your back."

"Lew, please. I'm serious. By careful, will you?"

"Sure," he said. And then his voice tightened with an antagonism he wished he could control, but couldn't. "Here he comes."

Sergeant Thomas Vallera nodded to his daughter and looked right through Lew McGee and slid into the patrol car, on the front seat, bringing with him a strong breath of mint and Jamaica rum. His heavy, dour face was flushed and sweaty. The collar of his uniform was unbuttoned, against regulations. He had a strong jaw, a mouth like an iron trap, uncompromising pale brown eyes that looked like amber, sometimes, the amber of a cat's eyes.

"Let's go, McGee," he said.

He never called him Lew, even though Lew had been seeing and taking Rose out for over two years.

"We ought to call in first," Lew said.

"No need, I spoke to Precinct. We're getting two extra cars in the area." The pale brown eyes slid sidewise to look at Lew. "Did you hear anything about tonight?"

"Tonight? No."

"You young college punks, you call yourselves cops—"

"What's tonight?" Lew said, ignoring the grating tone.

"By God, don't you ever keep your ears open?"

"I'm sorry, I didn't hear anything," Lew said evenly. He knew that a good cop depended on stool pigeons as part of the business, not thinking about the ethics or the morality of it, or even its decency. A cop couldn't make any headway at all without stoolies, and a cop, in return for information bought either with favors, leniency or brutality, protected his stoolie with everything he had. Sergeant Vallera had spent two-thirds of a lifetime building up his network of information. Lew McGee had just begun. He hadn't heard a whisper about anything on for tonight.

He turned east, not sure why, but maybe because he'd seen Johnny Broom and Stitch Pollard turn that way. They weren't in sight now. The street was full of shadows—the shadows of rundown bandboxes, old row houses of brick and brownstone with windows gaping, sometimes covered with cardboard or wooden slats in place of glass. And there were the shadows of people, old and young, sitting outside on the brownstone steps, gasping for air in the summer heat that clamped an iron, red-hot fist on the city.

"Comber told me," Vallera said suddenly.

Lew hated to ask. "What?"

"A rumble. Over at Sandor's Bowling Alley."

"That's where the Violets hang out, isn't it?"

"And the Lancers are going to pay them a visit. Maybe throw a few tenpins around." Vallera looked pleased. He popped a white mint into his mouth and chewed vigorously. His jaws rotated harshly, crushing the mint with small sounds of extermination. "We'll get 'em good tonight, the little bastards."

"What time is it set for?"

"Eleven, sharp."

"Why should Comber tell you about it?" Lew asked. "He makes money off the kids."

Vallera grinned. His face looked like a lion's head, hard and bony, angry. "That's a good question. Real good. Keep it up, and you might learn to be a cop some of these years, McGee. Why should Comber tell me? He tells me lots of things, but why should he offer this? This one is against his own interests, it seems."

Lew turned the car south on Front Street. There were factories, railroad sidings, a vast area of brick and rubble where a new housing development had cleared acres of ancient row houses. Good riddance, he thought.

Vallera said, "Talked to Johnny Broom's brother lately?"

"Pete? Pete's all right. A hard worker. Steady."

"Didn't say he wasn't. Just asked if you'd talked to him."

"No," Lew said and wondered why he felt uneasy again.

"We'll see him later. One other thing, McGee. No, two things. First, we're going to have company later. I got a call from the Hall. Courtesy to be extended to Mr. Henry Dexter Stephens. We pick him up a little after ten. The goddam do-gooder wants to watch how we handle a rumble. He's got the pull to snag a free ride with us."

Lew felt relieved. "You'll have to be careful, then."

Vallera laughed. "Careful? I got two fists and a club. A gun, if I need it. I'm going to smash 'em good, once and for all. Tonight I wipe up the gutters with that Johnny Broom and his punks. Tonight we're going to be all set and waiting for them."

Lew waited for the other thing.

Vallera said: "And about Rose."

"What about her?"

"You leave her alone, McGee. I'm getting tired of it. You ain't man enough for her and you never will be. I got plans for her that you'd only mess up. She's going places, my girl is, and it won't be with you, understand? She doesn't sweat out a life like her mother, a cop's wife, worrying all the time, living on stinking pay and living in a cheap, rundown house, trying all the time to be respectable and living with dirt."

Lew said coldly: "Is that the way you think about a cop's life?"

Vallera said: "I don't *think*—I know that's the way it is. No thinking about it."

"Then you ought to quit," Lew said. This time he couldn't control his anger. He had never let it get out of hand before, not in all these months of needling insults, being treated like an idiot child, condescended to and criticized and belittled and sneered at. All at once he was sick of it, full up to here with it. "You ought to quit," he said again. "You're not a good cop and you never were. You're drunk half the time we're on the trick, you've got half a dozen shakedown rackets going for you in the Jungle, you pal around with scummy racket men like Alois Comber—"

He stopped talking and felt his breath shake in his lungs.

Vallera said quietly: "I always figured you hate my guts, McGee."

"Yes."

"So why don't you turn me in?"

"You know why. I couldn't do that to Rose."

"So you're just a yellow, sniveling punk, after all. No better than Johnny Broom. A gutless wonder. That's the way I figured you," Vallera said in a quiet, deadly monotone, "and that's the way you are."

Lew couldn't say any more. Their hatred for each other built up like an explosive, expanding pressure inside the patrol car. He turned the windwing backwards so the hot, stale air smelling of human waste and rotting wood and ancient bricks hit him in the face.

It felt refreshing, after listening to Vallera.

Chapter Four

At nine o'clock it was fully dark, and the night breathed its heat over the Jungle.

Johnny walked quickly, always one step ahead of Stitch, feeling the dark drumbeats in the air. At Fifth Street he turned north and strode close to a leaning, wooden fence that enclosed a rubble-strewn lot. It was an old auto graveyard, and Stitch's wheels were here, hidden among the moldering, rusting wrecks of ancient vehicles.

"Wait up, man," Stitch panted. "Watch the speed limit."

"We've got things to do," Johnny said.

He paused at a point where the fence was braced by a four-by-four, looked up and down the street, and then leaped upward, his strong hands grabbing the top of the fence, pulling himself up and over to drop lightly on the brick-and-glass rubble on the other side. He didn't wait for Stitch to follow with his cumbersome movements.

The car belonged to Stitch, but Johnny had built it into what it was. Stitch had swiped the wheels two months ago, but like everything Stitch did, it was only a halfway effort, Johnny thought. He paused, wiping sweaty hands on his thighs, and considered the vague half shapes of wrecks that loomed all around him. Stitch had lifted an eight-year-old Pontiac that couldn't get up enough go to run away from a kid's pushmobile. But Johnny had worked on it as a labor of love, passing long hours on the motor, begging and wheedling the use of machine tools in Lovett's Garage, installing dual carburetors, grinding valves, changing the muffler, honing, polishing, cleaning, painting.

Stitch joined him at the car. He never drove it now

without Johnny's permission. It didn't look anything like the battered old relic he had swiped two months ago.

"Man, you did a job," Stitch breathed. "How fast do you think she'll go?"

"All we want," Johnny said.

"Faster than Vallera's heap?"

"A lot faster."

"Then we got it made, hey, man?"

"Why don't you shut up?" Johnny said tiredly.

Enough light filtered among the shadows of the auto graveyard for Johnny to inspect the car once more. He never tired of checking the gleaming, polished motor under the deceptive hood. Machinery, and working with fine precision tools, moved him into another world, almost. He had an instinct for such work, intuitive flashes that made him recognize just the right thing, with an ear for the music of oiled, polished parts sliding, clicking, compressing. He never talked about it. Not since the time he had tried to tell old Pete what he really wanted to do, and Pete had just drawn a blank on it. The words weren't there to explain how he felt about machines, not to anybody. Not that it would do any good if he could, he thought bitterly. Once, he had thought there might be a chance for him to go to some good technical school, like Drexel, say, and become an engineer. Work on rockets, stuff like that. It would've been wonderful. But thinking about it was useless. The money wasn't there, and nobody was just going to hand it to you, like, as a gift. It was stupid even to dream about it.

"Come on, Johnny," Stitch whined. The smell of his sweat was strong when he stood alongside Johnny. "You gonna stand there and look at the engine all night? You might think it was a dame, the way you play with it."

"You want a motor to run right, you got to take care of it," Johnny said. "More than if it was a piece."

"Like the way you take care of Flopsy?" Stitch said. He laughed, a thin grunting sound. "Her motor's gonna start missing, she gets sore waiting for you."

"She'll wait," Johnny said.

He closed the hood reluctantly.

"Can I drive, Johnny?" Stitch asked, wheedling again.

"Sure," Johnny said.

They went to Comber's place first. Alois Comber ran a cigar store down near Front and Susquehanna. It was dimly lighted behind its fly-specked windows, and a couple of Comber's boys loitered on the broken sidewalk, leaning against the brick wall or the old-fashioned gas lamp that still hadn't been replaced on this part of the city. Johnny made Stitch park the car up the street, and they walked the rest of the way.

Comber's boys were older than Johnny and Stitch, in their twenties, most of them, and their eyes filmed with cool contempt as Johnny went inside. The cigar store was long and narrow and dirty, and Comber sold candy and ice cream and cheap toys, as well as tobacco. There were rarely any customers, but Comber didn't need that kind of trade, anyway.

Alois Comber peddled pod and maybe horse, although Johnny wasn't sure about the bigger stuff, and he knew better than to ask or even to wonder about it. But he knew, with that instinctive Jungle knowledge, that Comber had his fat fingers in Precinct politics, and carried out orders for the numbers syndicate. Comber's wife, whom nobody had ever seen, owned a small trucking outfit. They said Comber's wife was chocolate brown and a crazy beauty, but nobody asked about that, either.

"Johnny, boy," Comber said. "Right on time."

"What did you expect?" Johnny asked.

"From a punk like you, a man never knows." Comber giggled, and his vast bulk shook under his sweaty silk shirt. "What's the matter with Stitch?"

"Nothin's the matter with me," Stitch said quickly.

"You look green, boy."

"I'm all right," Stitch muttered.

"You better be. Come on."

Comber left his place behind the glass cigar counter. Ordinarily, you never saw more of Alois Comber than his vast, sloping shoulders and round, bald head. He looked like a huge Buddha behind the counter, with his straight heavy black brows like a smear across pinpoint eyes in a suet face. But when he came out from behind the fly-blown display case, you saw that his paunch came in sharply just below his broad, brass-studded leather belt, and under that his legs were like pipe-stems, a bird's leg, wasted and thin, barely capable of supporting the monstrous weight of Comber's belly. His rump was flat and seemed to have no meat on it at all, following the pattern of his wasted legs in his white duck trousers.

They said Comber could handle that big leather belt better than a man could use a knife or a gun. Johnny didn't doubt it.

He followed Comber up a flight of back stairs, bathed in a dim brown light, and then down a hall to the rear of the building. Comber opened a door and went in, and Johnny followed. Stitch hesitated, then came in, too.

"We can talk here. Move your can, Flopsy," Comber rumbled.

"Hey," Stitch said. "You gave her some pod!" He

sounded outraged. "Can I have some, too, hey, Mr. Comber?"

The room stank of marijuana smoke. Johnny had tried the brown cigarettes once or twice, but he hadn't liked it, they only made him sick afterward, and he didn't use pod. But he didn't care if Flopsy reefed all she wanted to. She got stormy once in a while, but he always managed to handle her.

"Hello, man," Flopsy whispered dreamily.

Comber spoke to her sharply. "You all right, girl?"

"Just fine, Mr. Comber."

Flopsy lay on her back on the couch, her knees drawn up and her skirt slithered up around her hips. Her legs were fish-white and thin. She had tousled yellow hair, cut short so the ringlets hugged the shape of her head, and she had yellow-green eyes that usually looked as if no thought ever troubled her by passing through her mind.

"Johnny-O, sit down here," Flopsy said, patting the couch.

He stared at her coldly. "You didn't need pod tonight."

"How would you know? Comber was good to me. He gave me three sticks."

Stitch said eagerly: "Gimme one, huh, Flopsy?"

Flopsy looked at him. "You stink, you know that? You stink!"

Johnny saw Comber looking at him, and he turned away from the girl. Flopsy belonged to him, and he didn't like her coming up here to Comber's back room and laying around like that, half naked, but he didn't say anything about it. He'd fix her later for it. He didn't give a damn about Flopsy, anyway. She was stupid, she used too much pod, and at other times her hero-worship of him had a cloying quality that made him sick to his stomach.

"Johnny, are you going through with it?" Comber asked.

"Why, sure, Mr. Comber, sure. That's why I'm here."

"You got it all lined up? You know which cases we want, and where they are?"

"Yes, Mr. Comber. I went there yesterday." Johnny grinned. "I said I wanted a job."

"You're a good boy, Johnny," Comber nodded. "You do this right, and you can work for me again. Maybe on a regular basis. You want that?"

"Sure." *You fat son-of-a-bitch*, Johnny thought. *Some day you'll work for me.* He kept his face expressionless, however, and Comber looked away after a moment. "Anything you say, Mr. Comber."

Comber looked at him again with his tiny eyes like spiders crawling under the straight bars of his eyebrows. He wheezed and sweated. "I'm thinking about your brother. I'm worried about him."

"Pete won't give me any trouble."

"You're pretty sure about that?"

"I can handle Pete," Johnny said.

"I think you can—if you take this along—and if you use it, in case you need it."

Comber showed him the gun.

Johnny hadn't even thought about a gun. Maybe it was because Pete *was* involved in this, even though Pete didn't suspect a thing, and he knew he could always handle the dumb ox. So taking a gun along hadn't even occurred to him. He felt his mouth go dry, and he was angry with himself. He knew Comber was watching like a hawk. Flopsy and Stitch, who had been giggling on the couch, were suddenly silent. Silence closed in like a wall in the dingy, smelly room. Johnny knew it was a test, and he cursed this dryness in his throat and the squirm of fear and astonishment in him. He tried very hard not to let any of it show on his face.

"Well, don't you want it?" Comber whispered.

"Sure," Johnny said. "If you say so."

"I say so. So take it."

Johnny took the gun.

He had a funny feeling when he held its black, metallic weight in his hand. This was no home-made affair, no zip-gun, no toy crudely machined to spit a single slug which might or might not blow up in your hand. This was for real. It weighed a ton in his fingers. Yet it gave him the feeling that he was bigger than before, bigger than life itself. It was a strange, exciting feeling.

"You like the gun, Johnny?" Combers asked.

"Yeah. Sure."

"You can keep it. It's yours."

"Thanks, Mr. Comber," Johnny said.

Comber sighed and belched and shifted his lean flanks and swollen belly in the chair. His legs under the hanging white duck trousers looked skeletal, just bones. His eyes, like crawling black spiders again, watched Johnny.

"So what happens if Pete gets upset, like," Comber asked, "and you have to use that, Johnny? He's your brother. I'm takin' a big chance on you. We want those cases in that warehouse. I'm sendin' a truck around at eleven-forty sharp, you understand? It'll pull right up to the loading platform, and my boys will expect to see you comin' at them from the inside, unlockin' the gate so they can load up. You got to be quick and fast and no chicken business. But I can't help worryin' about you and your brother."

"It was my idea, wasn't it?" Johnny asked simply. "And where would we get if the watchman wasn't

Pete?"

"That's right. Are you sure he'll let you in?"

"I've gone into the warehouse with him before."

"He'll have a gun, too," Comber said. "All watchmen carry heat. Suppose he pulls it?"

"Then I'll use mine," Johnny said. "Don't worry about it."

"But I do worry," Comber said softly. He pursed his mouth and looked at Flopsy and Stitch, who were fooling around on the couch, and he made a little sucking noise that stopped and froze them. "Still, I guess I got to find out what kind of stuff you've got, Johnny-O. So good luck."

Johnny knew it was time to go.

He put the gun in his belt and pulled his tee-shirt over it. The heavy metal felt cold and oily against his waist. He hadn't figured on the gun at all.

It made a difference, but he didn't want to think about it.

"One more thing," Comber said.

Johnny turned and waited.

"I spoke to the blue men," Comber said. He grinned. "I told Vallera about your rumble."

One jolt after the other. He hadn't believed Stitch's rumor about a leak somewhere. Johnny felt as if he had been kicked in the stomach. He stared. Stitch gaped. Flopsy giggled.

"Why?" Johnny asked. His voice went high, and his single word had a thin, juvenile sound to it, and he cursed himself. "Why tell the blues?"

"To draw them away from the warehouse. Strategy, boy. You got to figure every angle. I'm trying to make it safe for you, Johnny-O."

"But the Lancers—"

"They're punk kids. Don't worry about them."

"But I called the rumble, I'm in charge of it.

They'll get it in the neck, those guys—"

"You're goin' on to bigger things, Johnny. Any objections?"

Johnny swallowed. He saw that Stitch was scared. He could smell Stitch's fear. For himself, he had the feeling that tonight he had started down a flight of dark stairs and couldn't stop himself until he reached the black, empty, terrible bottom. He pushed the feeling away and shook his head for the benefit of Comber's sharp spider eyes.

"No, no objection, Mr. Comber."

Chapter Five

The clock on the kitchen wall behind Rose Vallera read ten o'clock, exactly. She heard it click and whir like some giant red beetle clinging to the bright yellow paint. She looked at it but didn't see it. The exact hour didn't matter, she thought. It's all the hours of all the nights of all the years, never ending. It was a long, black whirlpool that sucked you down and never loosened its grip on you.

If only Lew could get along with Pa.

If only Lew could somehow finish and get his law degree and set up his practice.

If only they could be married.

She stared at the old, heavy, sticky-keyed typewriter on the porcelain-topped kitchen table before her. To her left, on the table, she had Lew's scribbled classroom lecture notes which she had offered to transcribe for him. It was easier for him to study from typewritten notes, but he didn't have the time to straighten them out himself between duty tours and classes.

But she was making too many errors in typing

tonight.

If she did a job like this for Mr. Stein, of Stein & Alder, on Locust Street, where she worked, she'd have been fired.

She didn't know why she was so nervous tonight.

It's the heat, she thought.

But it wasn't the heat. She was used to the heavy, suffocating stickiness of Philadelphia in mid-summer. She had lived with it every summer of her life.

Not the heat, but it would be nice if she and Lew could go to Atlantic City together for a couple of days. To swim and eat lobster down at that Inlet wharf, to walk on the Boardwalk with all its people and bright lights and amusement piers, feeling the ocean breeze cool on her face, smelling the rich smell of cigars and popcorn, and maybe step into one of the Boardwalk auction houses—just to look, not to buy, because everyone knew you couldn't trust some of those places.

It would be wonderful, just the two of them, being alone together. She didn't know how long she could be strong against the restless, wild yearnings she had when Lew held her in his arms.

But Lew had taken these summer extension courses, to help speed up the day he'd get his degree, and classes wouldn't be over for two weeks yet.

Maybe they'd go then.

If Pa didn't object.

And he would. Oh, he would.

She wondered if, like some parents she had read and heard about, Tom Vallera didn't want to lose her to *any* man. Not just Lew, but anyone who might come along and take her from here.

There were just the two of them now, and it had been that way for the last five years. Shortly after her mother died, Rose had tried to convince Tom that they ought to give up this big corner house and find some nice little apartment somewhere, maybe 'way uptown, in Ogontz or Oak Lane, or out in West Philadelphia even. But Tom wouldn't hear of it. This was his Precinct, and he didn't want to leave it. He wanted to keep on working here until the day he died. And he wanted Rose to stay with him until that happened.

She couldn't think of any other reason for the way Tom and Lew hated each other.

But because of their hatred, she was condemned to this house as if sentenced to prison, for an indeterminate number of years.

Maybe if Tom would stop drinking....

Maybe if Lew could explain to Tom how he felt about being a cop....

Maybe if she went to Lew and just kissed him quietly and said flat out that she wanted to get married now, right now, because she didn't want to wait and one of these nights she'd find she couldn't wait and they'd make a mistake....

Maybe.

Rose got up and walked through the darkened house to the front room, the old "parlor." She could remember how it had been when she was little, and her mother was still alive: the smell of lemon oil, furniture polish, the luster of the mahogany interior shutters over the triple curved windows in the corner, in the false turret that went up to the third floor. She remembered the crisp fold and fall of curtain drapes. She walked to the tiny vestibule, the old foyer with its Victorian interior doors of colored, leaded glass. And the heavy pottery umbrella stand, where she always dropped her skates or her ball, her jacks and dolls, when she ran home from school or from play. But it didn't do any good to remember these things. You can't bring the past back, just by remembering. It was only an illusion.

She didn't turn on any lights when she went upstairs. Somehow it didn't seem safe—

The thought startled her. She had never felt unsafe in this house before. It was like a rock; Pa had made it secure, and nothing could ever touch it, no matter what happened in the neighborhood.

Yet she stopped and stood still in a pool of quiet, unaccustomed fear.

Like a sullen drumbeat, the heat of the night pulsed in and around her.

Nerves, Rose thought.

She decided to take a shower. A cool shower would make her feel better. And then she'd finish typing Lew's notes.

She pulled the cotton dress up over her head and hung it up carefully to keep the humid heat from creasing it, and then she undressed to the skin and stepped into the high old tub and drew the shower curtain around her.

She looked down at herself and saw her body.

All at once she remembered Stitch Pollard. She knew him. She had known him since he was born.

She remembered how he had looked at her, with insolence and arrogance and the hunger in his rebellious eyes.

Suddenly she felt as if she had to dress again. She felt as if she couldn't get her clothes on fast enough.

At ten-thirty, Tom Vallera said: "We'll wait here, McGee. This is as good a spot as any."

It was the first time he had spoken in half an hour. Lew dutifully pulled the patrol car toward the curb and set the brake, although he left the motor running.

Vallera sat in the back seat with Henry Dexter

Stephens, chewing a fresh mint with that slow, meticulous, crushing rotation of his jaws. Stephens leaned forward and tapped Lew's shoulder, and his thin, autocratic voice, edged with sharp interest, spoke directly into his ear.

"Is that the place?"

"Sandor's Bowling Alley? Yes, sir," Lew said.

"It looks quiet enough."

"Some of these fighting gangs of hoodlums," Vallera said, "work with almost military precision, Mr. Stephens. Their organization is detailed and their discipline is hard and tough. Eleven o'clock will bring 'em as they planned."

"If you're so sure there's going to be a rumble," Stephens objected, "why can't we send men in there to stop it now, before it starts?"

"They'd just move someplace else, Mr. Stephens."

"But if you arrested the leaders—"

"On what charges?" Vallera's voice was heavy with contempt. He didn't conceal his hostility. "You pull some of those punks in without a case, and you get their parents, the priests, the psychiatrists, the magistrates, and every social worker in the city down on your neck."

Stephens said bluntly: "Including me and the Governor's Commission?"

"Yes, sir," Vallera said. "Including you."

"But it seems to me, in a case like this—"

"Just picture how you'd react, Mr. Stephens, if you weren't here with us tonight, right on the spot, and if you opened your paper tomorrow morning and read where we threw half a dozen of these kids into the clink, maybe had to cuff them around a little. You'd be paying for the lawyers yourself, to spring 'em—"

Stephens said: "Your attitude seems unreasonably

hostile, sergeant."

"I've got reasons to feel that way."

Lew kept studying the bowling alley on the corner. It was really a triple corner, where an avenue slanted across the neat, geometric gridwork of Philadelphia's streets. The traffic light made splashes of red and green light that over-ran the patrol car in alternate waves. Then the neon sign that read *Sandor's Bowling* would come on, a hissing, spitting yellow.

The intersection seemed quiet. Now and then a car passed, and occasionally the swift rumble of a trolley sounded from behind their parking place. The entrance to the bowling alleys was on the side, beyond several dim store windows, and you mounted a long, steep flight of wooden stairs with steel treads. Up there, Sandor sold beer and sandwiches and cokes. The crashing din of falling tenpins echoed now and then down the dark side street where they waited.

Lew had taken Rose here two or three times on the rare nights he found himself free. Rose was a good bowler, and she beat Lew as often as he won over her. Sandor's was respectable enough, a neighborhood recreation center, and Sandor himself had often complained about the way the Violet gang hung out on the premises.

"How many extra cars have you called into this?" Stephens asked.

"Just two," Vallera said.

"Will that be enough?"

"We'll make it do."

"You're anxious to get this Johnny Broom, aren't you?"

"Well, sure," Vallera said. "He's a trouble-maker, and he's the warlord of the Lancers. He'll wind up in the chair, I'll bet anything on it. But he isn't going to make trouble in my Precinct. Not if I have to—not if I can help it."

Two or three boys drifted to the entrance under Sandor's neon sign and went upstairs to the bowling alley. The traffic light changed to red and then to green again. Vallera whistled a tuneless sound through his teeth.

"Thing is," Vallera said, "we may not stay around here after the rumble starts. I think it's a phony."

Lew was startled by this. "Why?" he asked.

"You ain't thinking tonight, McGee," Vallera said. "A good cop has to be suspicious. You can't believe everything you hear. You got to look it over from top to bottom and from every direction, and even then, you tell yourself not to believe what you see. Or hear."

"Meaning Comber handing you this on a platter?" Lew asked.

Vallera didn't bother to answer.

Stephens sat back in the patrol car and lit a cigarette. A trolley went by behind them, rumbling and hissing. It was hot in the patrol car. Lew sweated under his uniform coat. He thought he heard the distant rolling of thunder, but it could have been only the heavy, heated pulse of angry blood in his ears.

Mike Tarrant saw the patrol car when he saw the corner. He stopped and looked at its silent bulk parked in the shadows of the side street, and a minor explosion of fear burst silently in him. He retreated quickly, silently. Fortunately, he had come upon the car from the back, and unless one of the cops saw him in the rear-vision mirror, he was safe. Not that he had anything to worry about, from a cop, unless he was picked up for questioning. And there was no reason why they should do that.

A few minutes later he was amused to spot the

other two squad cars parked strategically in an orbit around Sandor's Bowling Alley. So they knew about the rumble, or suspected. Mike wondered if he should seek out Johnny Broom and tell him. He decided not to. He didn't owe Johnny anything. It would be fun to watch what happened later. And meanwhile, he didn't have much time to start his evening's entertainment rolling.

He was a part of the night, sliding along the hot dark shadows of the street. The people he passed, sitting on their front steps, gasping for a breath of air, paid no attention to him. Nor did he look at any of them twice. They made him think of Jane's tropical fish—that time he had emptied the water in the tank and stood there to watch them die, their gills working spasmodically. Afterwards, he told her it was an accident, and he got her other fish to take the place of those he had killed. The people sitting on their front steps were no more than fish to him now.

He felt impatient to begin. There was a certain danger in wandering alone through the Jungle like this, but it was a danger he had tasted before and enjoyed. He felt alive down to his fingertips, filled with a secret exultation. A rhythm beat through his mind, sometimes forming words, sometimes without substance at all, a cool, smooth rhythm formed of notes and phrases and senseless yearnings.

"Angry, angry ... bop ... bop ... goddam old lady always snooping, grouping, telling, yelling ... bop ... stupid eyes watching ... fish, dish ... watch her walk, legs swinging ... bop ... come, oh come in, make me angry ... step across the mud ... bop ... step across the blood ... bop...."

The night was dull, a charcoal smear over the streets and alleys. Nothing was going to happen. He paused for a moment outside a corner taproom. Some of the men in there wore only skivvie shirts. It was a dirty, dingy place. Some kids ran screaming past him, howling into the night. From the house on the other side of the street came a blast of cool music, a man's shout, and an even greater volume from the radio. Mike walked around the corner to the ladies' entrance to the taproom—Pennsylvania law requiring different doorways to the same bar for the opposite sexes. A woman sat on the adjacent stone steps, fanning herself with a paper fan.

"Hello, man."

Mike peered at her, trying to make her out in the dimness. A round, cow face, something like Jane's, and a thin, sweaty cotton dress that clung here and there to her soft woman's curves. He felt hatred swim up in his mind like a predatory fish seeking minnows on the surface.

"You a new kid around here?" the woman asked.

"You think I'm a kid?" Mike asked.

"Oops. Sorry, man. Just my way of speaking. We're all children, man, children lost, strayed and stolen." She hiccupped and grinned. "So you think you're a man?"

"I think so," Mike said flatly.

"You look real nice. Real nice. A nice boy."

"You like me?" Mike asked.

"Sure. Siddown. You got the price of a drink?"

"Maybe."

Her eyes were professionally sly. "I drink a lot, man."

"I can pay for it."

She sighed and stood up, made vague, pathetic gestures with her hands to smooth the wrinkled dress. She looked down at him, and her round face twisted strangely. "I'm gonna hate myself, you know? I don't usually do this. But the old man, he's out of work, won't look for nothin' to do, and I got two kids. You mind if I tell you that? We're all children, y'know, and nobody should mind a couple extra kids."

"I don't mind," Mike said. He hated her. This one would do. "Let's go somewhere," he said.

"I can't take you to my place. The old man is there."

"The alley, then," Mike said. He felt impatient.

The woman giggled, then hiccupped and looked as if she were going to cry. "Can't wait, huh? I'll bet you—"

"Just shut up and let's go," Mike said.

"I want two bucks," she said.

"You'll get it."

"I don't usually do this," she whined, following him. "But I don't know what else I can do, do you? My soul is clean, my soul is the soul of a little child in the wilderness."

"Yeah, sure," Mike said.

"You don't believe that?" she asked angrily. She plucked at his arm. "Hey, where we going?"

"This will do," Mike said.

They were at the entrance of a dark alley, a black slot bisecting the block of rundown row houses. When he paused and looked up and down the street, he heard the distant wail and hoot of a switch engine in the railroad yards over to Frankford. He didn't see anybody watching him. When he gestured to the woman, she slipped past him into the darkness of the alley.

"Pay me first," she said.

He took her arm. "Let's go in a little farther."

She hesitated, then went ahead. A cat scurried out of their way, hissing and spitting, clawed up the board fence and vanished. There were trash cans, wooden crates and a thin stream of thick, viscous water in the middle of the narrow passage. It was almost totally black, here, but Mike could see the woman's moon face turned toward him, bland and stupid and anonymous.

"Hey," she said, "you sure you got the money?"

"Right here."

He gave her two dollars, their hands fumbling in the dark. He saw the flash of white from her thigh as she bent forward to tuck the bills in her stocking. Excitement boiled up in him. She straightened, smiling.

"You're a nice kid ... you got nice hair...."

She reached and ran her fingers through his hair.

He hit her then. A strangled, coughing sound, like a snort, came from her. He hit her again. A fury seized him. His exultation roared. She made frantic, scrabbling motions on the cement paving of the alley, trying to get away from him. For just an instant he saw her face clearly in the glowing radiance of a car that passed the mouth of the alley. He saw her utter astonishment, her stupid amazement, her fear that went far beyond any understanding of what was happening to her.

"Jane ..." he gasped. "Mother—Jane...."

"Please...."

He kicked her. He didn't want to stop. He felt stronger, darker, bigger than the night. The heat of the summer flashed and exploded and tingled along every nerve ending in his body....

When he stopped, he was drenched with sweat.

The woman lay still.

He didn't know if she was dead or not. He didn't care.

He bent over her, reluctantly feeling the smoothness of her fleshy thigh and took back the two dollars he had handed her.

Then he walked out of the alley.
He walked as if he trod on air.
He went looking for Johnny Broom.

Chapter Six

The Lancers were waiting for Johnny and Stitch at their meeting place on Sixth Street. There were twenty-two members, and they ranged in age from eighteen to fourteen. Six of them were girls, including Flopsy, and the girls were difficult to tell from the boys, their hair close-cropped, wearing the same red tee-shirts and dungaree outfit that was the uniform of the Lancers.

A row of condemned and vacated houses on Sixth Street surrounded them, waiting for the wrecking cranes to level the block for the new housing development. Each house had identical cellar windows opening on the pavement, three feet wide, two feet high. In most of the houses, the sashes had been smashed or removed, and Johnny entered the meeting place through the broken hole gaping just above the sidewalk level, sliding in feet first, dropping down on the rickety table just below it, in what had been the coal bin. It was dark here. He groped his way forward to the makeshift door and opened it. Stitch squeezed through after him, and they were in the lighted club room, where the twenty-two Lancers waited.

The air in the club room was thick with cigarette smoke, and the cloying odor of pod. There was a general murmured chorus of greetings, and the Judge stood up.

"You're late, Johnny," the Judge said.

"Only a minute."

"We're all set to go."

"Sit down," Johnny said.

The Judge remained standing. His name was Hank Jennings, and of all the members of the Lancers, Hank was the only one who had opposed Johnny's election as warlord. He was the oldest, well beyond eighteen, and he had accepted the secondary post as judge for matters of disciplinary decision only reluctantly. In a way, the Judge was held in more fear by the Lancers than Johnny. His decisions in matters of argument were arbitrary but inflexible.

He was bigger than Johnny, well-muscled, with the pale white hair and eyes of an albino. Johnny knew he had gone beyond the use of marijuana and was taking the Big H, and when the horse talked in him, you didn't talk back. Johnny met the pale eyes and saw that Jennings was riding high, higher then he should tonight, out of this world. There was a dreamy quality in the Judge's face that he didn't like. Jennings cropped his white hair so short that it looked only like bleached fuzz on the bullet shape of his skull.

"I said, sit down," Johnny repeated.

"We've been talking about this rumble you called," the Judge said. He smiled dreamily. He didn't sit down. "We want to know why you called it, is all."

"The Violets got it coming to them," Johnny said. "And you have no right to question my decisions in this. This is my jurisdiction."

"Sure, Johnny. But we like to understand it."

For the first time, Johnny sensed the challenging hostility toward him in the clubroom. It had never happened before. Stitch took a step backward and stood behind him. Flopsy had remained in the car outside. The challenge stood like something ugly and implacable between Johnny and the Judge.

The members stirred restlessly, watching and waiting. Their eyes gleamed. One of the girls giggled. They were all armed, he saw, ready to obey his orders. Switch-blades and gravity knives, brass-studded belts, lengths of galvanized pipe. Georgie Davers had a zip-gun. Angela was twirling brass knuckles in her big hands, whistling soundlessly. Johnny saw the way they watched him, like animals ready to pounce and rip and claw, turning on a wounded member. *Loyalty*. His mind spit the word out angrily. They'd be happy to stomp him to death, and they'd do it with glee, if they had the nerve, if he backed down. He felt better about what he was going to do tonight. To hell with them all, he thought. They'd get only what they deserved.

But first he had to take care of the Judge.

The Judge was high on horse and dangerous. He waited with the patience of a man to whom time had become meaningless in the way-up-there of heroin. Jennings outweighed him by fifteen pounds, stood half a head taller. The rest of the gang was afraid of the albino, just because of his looks.

Johnny spoke quietly. "You all know what to do. We're going to Sandor's. We go in one and two at a time, but quick, so they don't catch half of us on the street and the other half in the bowling alley. We tear the place apart. You wait until I walk over to Davey O'Hara, their chief. When I make my move, you make yours. Ten minutes, that's all. You watch the clock over the middle of the alleys. When Stitch blows the whistle, we all get out fast."

"You got your wheels, Johnny?" the Judge drawled.

"Yes."

"And the rest of us run, walk, or crawl?"

"The best you can," Johnny said. "I'll take as

many as can pile into the car."

"You still don't explain why we meet 'em on their ground. Why not neutral territory? They know Sandor's like I know my fist."

One of the girls added to the remark, using a filthy expression, and giggled. Johnny didn't look at her. He knew it was Angela, jingling the brass knuckles.

"I figured it," Johnny said. "You get no other explanation. Let's go."

Nobody moved.

They waited for the Judge.

The Judge laughed and said, "Nuts, Johnny."

Johnny cut him down. He did it quickly, murderously, with no warning. He didn't even think about it himself, when he moved. He was hoping that the horse that dreamed in the Judge's veins would make his reactions slow and off-center, and he was right. He used his fists coldly and brutally, not enjoying it, but doing it as a job that had to be done quickly and efficiently. Jennings was like an engine, hard to stop. Blood flowed from his nose, and several broken teeth lay on the floor. Johnny felt the other's huge fist finally connect, slamming into his ribs with the force of a telephone pole. He fell back against the wall.

Most of the Lancers were on their feet now. He saw them through a momentary haze, their faces like eager animals, mouths open, eyes glistening, hungry for a kill. He pulled himself together. The Judge was straightening, grinning through his bloody, broken mouth. Johnny's shirt was torn, hanging in ribbons from his left shoulder, and there was blood running down his arm. He didn't even know how it had happened. Fear touched him, and the fear gave him extra strength. He cut down the Judge for keeps, threw him against Angela, who wailed and screamed and crawled out of the way.

The Judge didn't move after that.

There was silence in the clubroom, marked only by the queer rasp of the albino's breathing.

Then there was a sigh that came simultaneously from all the Lancers.

Johnny straightened. He looked at his shoulder and saw that the Judge's fingers had clawed a triple gash in his flesh. But it didn't hurt. He took out the gun Comber had given him and walked across the room toward the Judge's sprawled figure. He had kept the gun in his pocket until now. None of them had known about it.

Another sigh went up from the Lancers.

Angela whispered.

"Don't, Johnny.... He didn't know what he was saying."

Johnny paused. The gun felt like a hot, live animal in his fist. It felt good. He wanted to use it. His hatred almost spilled over in a red tide that left him shaking and trembling.

He said, "All right, then. Anybody else want to question my decisions?"

Nobody spoke.

"Then let's go," he said.

He felt better about his deal with Comber now. He felt just fine.

At ten minutes to eleven, Sandor put in a telephone call to Precinct, calling for the police. He was a small, bald, excitable man, and excitement was bad for him, considering his heart condition. He felt his heart clamor with crazy urgency as he spoke to the desk sergeant and heard the cop's quiet, reassuring words.

"You know about it already?" Sandor yelled.

Then he lowered his voice, because he didn't want it to be heard through the glass door of his office. Tenpins crashed like thunder in the bowling alleys, and he saw the flicker of red from a Lancer's shirt, a clot of red down at the far end of the alleys where the Lancers had congregated. "So where are the cops? My God, I need some protection!"

"Don't you worry about a thing, Mr. Sandor," the desk sergeant said placatingly. "It's all under control."

"You ever see these kids in a rumble? They go crazy—"

"Just take it easy, Mr. Sandor."

Sandor hung up. He didn't know whether to believe the Precinct or not, but he told himself he had to; he had to stay calm. The familiar squeezing pain began in his chest, and he fumbled in his shirt pocket for the plastic box of pills and got one out in shaking fingers, popped it into his mouth and crushed it.

Damned, crazy kids.

A man tries to run a decent place—

Then he heard somebody scream.

Johnny had sent Stitch and Flopsy drifting out of the place a moment before. None of the other Lancers had questioned him. Maybe they hadn't even noticed. Then he had wandered over to Davey O'Hara, the chief of the Violets. Some factory club from Kensington was running a play-off tournament with a Roxbury outfit in the middle alleys, and Johnny skirted the sweaty, excited factory men to reach the Violet alleys. He didn't worry about adult interference in the joint once the rumble started. They'd be afraid to mess into it.

O'Hara saw him coming and looked surprised. Maybe O'Hara knew the rumble had been tipped to the cops and hadn't really expected the Lancers to show up. Johnny decided it didn't matter.

Everything was set, and it was too late to change things.

There were more than thirty Violets, including their girls. Most of them went on bowling, but some of the muscle stopped and bunched up behind O'Hara. They stood a little distance away, though, to let O'Hara talk to Johnny alone.

"Make like a bird," O'Hara said. "Go pull your cork in somebody else's yard. This ain't the night for it."

Johnny grinned. The skin on his face felt tight, but he could feel the sag and pull of the gun in his pocket. "We got a date, haven't we?"

"It's cancelled," O'Hara said. "The blues are in on it."

"You afraid of the blues?"

O'Hara said something that was drowned out in the momentary crash and thunder of tenpins in the middle alleys. Davey O'Hara was short and chunky, with a broken nose and dark blue eyes and wisely carved lips. He made the mistake of bending over one of the alley ramps to pick up a sixteen-pound ball. Before he could lift it, Johnny chopped down on the back of his neck, bent him backward over the channel by which the balls were returned from the head of the alley, and then punched down as hard as he could on O'Hara's taut belly.

His attack on O'Hara, chief of the Violets, was the signal for bedlam. Violence was unleashed like the sudden clapping thunder of a summer storm. For an instant, the lone rumble and crash of a ball going down one of the middle alleys was the only sound. Then Angela screamed. It was the scream Sandor heard. The two gangs came together with a shock of cursing, thudding, shouting blows.

"Come on, Johnny!" Stitch yelled.

Johnny threw one of the bowling balls into a knot of on-rushing Violets and stepped back. O'Hara was trying to crawl away down one of the alleys. Johnny ignored him, felt Stitch tug impatiently at his arm, and let the Lancers charge past him into the thick of the Violet men. He heard Sandor yelling something and turned to see the little proprietor clutch his chest and stagger through his office door. Johnny turned that way with Stitch at his heels.

Behind him, the sounds of the rumble lifted to a crescendo. The Lancers had run across the alleys, grabbing up bowling pins and balls. The Violets, forewarned, were ready and waiting for them. Johnny looked back and saw Georgie Davers go down when a tenpin hit him in the face. Somebody else snatched up Davey's zip-gun. Angela kept on screaming and clawing, fighting one of the Violet girls.

He didn't look back again. He was faintly conscious of a high, thin whistling as he plunged into Sandor's office. The little proprietor was leaning over his desk, clawing at his chest. His face looked strangely convulsed and unnatural.

"Hey," Johnny gasped. "Which way out?"

"You—you devils—"

"Come on, Pop, or you get slugged, you hear? How do I get out?"

"The police are here—you can't—"

Sandor coughed and gagged. He was trying to lift one of his pills to his mouth, but the effort was too much for his shaking hands. Johnny hesitated for a moment, watching him with cold eyes. He heard the rush of pounding feet past the office door. The thin whistling sound was repeated. A cop's whistle. He sweated, felt a clutch of panic. Stitch, at the door behind him, whimpered.

"We're getting clobbered, Johnny-O."

"Shut up," Johnny said.

Sandor fell to the floor behind the desk. Johnny hadn't put a hand on him. The pills went rolling across the small carpet. Johnny ran around the desk, stepped over Sandor, and yanked open a door in the rear of Sandor's office. Shouts and screams came from the bowling alley. The triumphant war yell of the Violets was dominant.

The door behind Sandor's office opened into a long, dark corridor that paralleled the bowling alleys.

"Come on," Johnny snapped to Stitch.

He ran down the corridor. It led to the area behind the alleys where the automatic pin-setting machines operated. It was a big, dusty place, gloomily lighted, echoing strangely. Johnny skidded to a halt. Stitch joined him.

"Johnny, it's awful—I'm scared—"

"Then go back," Johnny rasped. He was filled with fury. "Go back, chicken!"

"I can't. The cops jumped all our guys—didn't you see?"

"Who cares? We got to keep moving."

"But, Johnny—"

Johnny whirled in rage and saw the paralysis of fear on Stitch. He suddenly spoke in a lower tone. "Where are those stairs in the back you told me about?"

"Over there, Johnny."

"Come on, then. We waste more time, we're in the soup, too."

His quieter tone reassured Stitch. They ran for a narrow back stairway that led to a rear entrance to the bowling alleys. Nobody was in sight, and no one appeared to stop them as they clattered down the worn, wooden treads to the street level.

Outside, the sounds of the rumble were muted, as if completely disconnected from them. The street was hot and silent, and dark. Johnny turned left, began to run, then slowed down to a walk as a police car flashed past the intersection, siren howling like an animal lost in the night. Stitch was breathing in great, shuddering gasps, as if he could no longer control the wild pumping of his lungs.

"It's all right now, Stitch," Johnny said quietly. "Let's find Flopsy and the car."

"I was never so scared, Johnny—"

"It's all right. I tell you!" Johnny repeated. "Come on, we've got a lot to do. We're hardly started."

"I don't feel so good, Johnny—"

"You'll feel worse if we get caught hanging around here."

Stitch responded to the whip-threat of further danger. He trotted doggedly after Johnny, up a long, dark alley, turning left at the next street, circling the block, and coming up on the dark silhouette of the hot-rod where Flopsy waited. Johnny saw the car with a vast feeling of relief. Everything was working out. They were only a few minutes late, that was all. It would be all right.

He ran over to the car and opened the front door.

Flopsy seemed to be asleep, curled up on the seat in a tight, pale ball of disheveled dress and skinny white legs.

Mike Tarrant sat behind the wheel.

Chapter Seven

The Keystone Fidelity Bonded Warehouse stood beyond the railroad spurs in Frankford, several blocks from Rising Sun Avenue. It was a long brick building occupying most of the block, with archaic brick towers at each end, a cobblestone street crossing the freight spur at one end, and a long truck-loading ramp at the other.

Mike Tarrant turned the Pontiac at the corner, and they bumped over the railroad tracks and drove the length of the huge, silent warehouse. Most of the windows on the second floor were dark. On the ground floor there was a light in one window under the truck-loading tower where Johnny knew his brother, Pete, would sit most of the night, reading magazines and drinking coffee between regular rounds of punching in at stations with his time clock.

"There's Comber's truck," Stitch said suddenly.

Johnny didn't see it at first, then its bulk suddenly took on definition, parked beyond the railroad tracks alongside a high board fence. Its lights were off, but the motor throbbed quietly as they went by. Johnny couldn't see the men in the cab, but he hoped they weren't too impatient. He was only ten minutes late.

"Park around the corner," he told Mike.

Mike obeyed quietly. Flopsy woke up when they stopped. She looked at Mike and made a gagging noise and then looked around and said: "What goes on?"

"You stay in the car," Johnny said. "You and Stitch, and we will go in and open the loading door."

Stitch said: "Fine by me."

Johnny got out, and Mike walked silently by his side. Crossing the railroad spur, they could see the bulk of Comber's truck waiting far down the street.

There was a long, weed-grown driveway, unused, behind the warehouse. The warehouse wall on this side was blank, windowless, solid brick; on the other side of the weedy driveway was a high wire fence guarding the railroad spur. Blue light washed down the driveway from the mercury vapor lamps of a nightshift working in a paper-box factory in the next block. There was a smell of decay in the hot, stale air.

"Let me see the gun," Mike asked.

"You don't have to see it," Johnny said.

"You going to use it?"

"I won't have to."

Mike's narrow, predatory face looked strange in the odd blue light that bathed them as they walked down the driveway. In this industrial area of Frankford there were few row houses, and only drifting shadows that orbited around the dimly lighted, sleazy taprooms that inevitably occupied the corner spots. Johnny felt uncomfortable with Mike. Stitch called Mike a creep, and Johnny had to acknowledge that he felt uneasy with him. It had been startling to find Mike casually lolling in the car when they got away from Sandor's. The guy was everywhere, a loner who liked to prowl in the shadows, seeing everything, knowing everything that went on, coming and going with the night. Johnny wished he knew more about Mike.

Johnny paused. "You know this neighborhood, Mike?"

"Sure."

"You come from around here, then?"

"No."

"Where *do* you come from?"

"What difference does it make?" Mike said. His grin was sardonic. His eyes looked hot and crazy, glazed with excitement. He didn't seem to know fear, like Stitch. Johnny knew he could be trusted to follow and help, if help was needed. But he still felt uneasy.

"You don't talk like us," Johnny said. "You try to, but you don't. You come from a fancy family, I figure. You come down here for kicks, is that it?"

"You're very observant," Mike said.

"That's what I mean. Talk like that. Who are your folks?"

"Nobody you'd want to know. You going to ring that bell or not? We haven't got all night, you said."

They stood in the doorway of the office entrance, where Johnny had been admitted on past occasions by Pete. There was a small bell marked *Night Watchman* in the wall beside the door, and Johnny drew a breath and thumbed it. He heard a faint pealing far inside the dark, huge building. He rang again.

Mike grinned. "Your brother must be asleep on the job."

Johnny rang a third time.

At eleven-fifteen, two blocks away from the Keystone Warehouse, Sergeant Vallera signaled to Lew McGee to halt the patrol car. Lew asked no questions. He knew the old man was up to something, but Vallera kept hugging it to himself as if it were a national secret. And with Henry Dexter Stephens riding as an observer in the prowlie, Lew felt under some restraint to say what he really thought about it.

Vallera spoke quietly. "You see that truck? Over by the fence? That belongs to Comber's wife. Now, I wonder why it should be parked way over there? You got any ideas about that, McGee?"

"Some," Lew admitted.

"I confess I don't understand this," Stephens said

uneasily. "You're out of your territory, aren't you, Sergeant? You're not in your own Precinct patrol anymore."

"No, we ain't," Vallera said thickly.

"I don't want to seem to interfere in the performance of your duty, sergeant," Stephens said. "But it seems to me that you have had knowledge both of the rumble—which you completely ignored the moment you spotted young Johnny Broom leaving that bowling alley—and you also have foreknowledge of something about to happen here. Wouldn't you say your duty as a police officer is a preventive one as well as punitive?"

"I just do my job the way I figure it's best," Vallera said.

"You're out to get this Johnny Broom, aren't you?"

"He's a bad one," Vallera admitted.

"There are no bad youngsters. Only a bad society, and bad parents."

"This ain't no time for theories, Mr. Stephens. You'll see what I mean in a minute."

But Stephens was insistent. An edge of thin anger had entered his cultured voice. "You have knowledge of a crime about to be committed here by Johnny Broom, haven't you?"

"I heard a rumor, sure."

"So you followed him and you're going to sit by until the deed is done, and *then* arrest him for it."

Vallera reacted to Stephen's cold criticism with a thick anger of his own. "It's all very well for you people from Society Hill to theorize about crime, Stephens, but you don't know these young hoods. And it ain't just Johnny Broom, either. It's Alois Comber I'm after, too. What happens if I move in now and stop whatever Broom is up to? You think I can put the arm on Comber, too? He's got a battery of high-priced legal talent that could cost me my badge for false arrest."

"But that boy's life can be ruined because of your self-concern for your badge," Stephens protested. He suddenly elbowed the door of the patrol car open and got out on the pavement. He stood for a moment staring at the dark loom of the warehouse two blocks away. "If you won't do anything to prevent that boy from making a grievous error, I will."

"Stephens!" Vallera's voice was a harsh, angry whisper.

"Let me remind you, you're here with me as a courtesy. Get back in the car and don't interfere."

"Will you just sit here and wait for the crime to be committed, then?"

Lew spoke up for the first time. He tasted bitterness in his throat. "That's the way the sergeant operates, Mr. Stephens."

Stephens turned his narrow, aristocratic head to look at Lew. "Do you agree with this method, McGee?"

"No," Lew said. "But I have to take orders."

"Well, I don't. I'm going in there," Stephens decided.

Vallera's voice shook with anger. "You mess this up and I'll see to it the papers crucify you, Stephens. You don't know what you're walking into—"

Stephens didn't bother to reply.

Pete was surprised and pleased to see Johnny. His round, placid face considered Mike with some uneasiness, but he opened the door of the warehouse wide to let them in. "Oh, it's you, Johnny. Look, you're too late if you're here to ask about that job I tried to get for you."

"We didn't come here for a job, Petey-O," Mike said. "We—"

"Let me handle this," Johnny interrupted.

Pete Broom looked from one boy to the other. "Who's your friend, Johnny?"

"Just a guy."

"Look, I'm not supposed to let anybody in here. You know that. If you didn't come about the job, what are you here for?" Pete's voice suddenly lifted in concern. "You in trouble, Johnny? Did you and the Lancers get in a jam with the cops? Is that why you're here?"

"You're the one who's in trouble, Petey-O," Mike said calmly. "Show him the gun, Johnny boy."

"The gun—"

There was no help for it. Johnny hadn't wanted it quite this way. He knew that Mike had deliberately pushed the thing, trapping him into a quick play. He took out the gun Comber had given him and saw Pete's face change to one of dumb incredulity. *The stupid ox*, Johnny thought.

"Johnny, what—"

"We want your keys, Pete." Johnny felt as if a hand was squeezing the breath out of his lungs. "The keys to the big doors on the truck-loading ramp."

"You crazy? Put that gun away!"

"Don't you get it?" Mike said softly. "We're helping ourselves to a few items in the warehouse."

Pete turned fiercely to Mike. "Who are you? Where do you come into this? Did you talk Johnny—"

Johnny said: "Petey-O. The keys, huh?"

There was a pause. The anteroom to Pete's own office as night watchman was dimly lighted. There was no sound except the labored incredulous breathing sound that Pete made. His eyes jumped from one boy to the other. Johnny couldn't understand the look in them when they fixed on him. There was something wrong. Pete wasn't paying any attention at all to the gun Johnny had. He didn't even look at it. Maybe he didn't even know it was there, anymore.

Time was running out.

Johnny felt as if a drum was beating in his chest. His hand, holding the gun, felt hot and wet and slippery. He licked his lips.

"Pete, we don't want to hurt you. Just do as I say—"

"No, by God, no!" Pete shouted. "You're just a crazy kid! Who put you up to this? Johnny, I'm your *brother*—"

His voice spiraled up in a loud, echoing alarm.

"Shut up," Johnny said. "Give me the keys."

"Johnny, you'll be arrested—you're the kid I—I promised Ma I'd see to it you didn't get in trouble—don't make me—"

Mike laughed. "He talks a lot, Johnny boy."

Pete's round face suddenly hardened. Johnny had never seen it happen before. Always, Pete was slow and placid and muscle-bound, a big, clumsy, good-natured, easy-to-fool guy.

This was different. This was a man he didn't know. A stranger with hard, bitter eyes, a disillusioned mouth.

And Pete jumped for the red alarm button in the wall behind him.

It was Mike who stopped him. Johnny held the gun in his hand, but it was like a rock, frozen there. He had told Comber he could use it; he had told himself he would and could use it. But he couldn't. Not on Pete.

Mike laughed and dived for Pete and slapped his

arm down and away from the red alarm button, and then he did something to Pete so fast that Johnny couldn't see what it was. But a thin scream of agony came from Pete, and he went reeling toward the door, bent over, his face grey and lined like the face of an old man.

Johnny ran to him. Pete hit the wall as if he was blind and fell to his knees, bending over, groaning.

"Pete, I told you to give me the keys—"

Mike came over and ripped them from the belt Pete wore.

"I got them."

"Pete, listen—" Johnny whispered.

Pete looked at him with eyes of hate. "Get away from me."

"Let me help you up."

"Get—*away!*"

Johnny wanted to touch him, to lift him, anyway. Somewhere deep inside him a voice cried, *The dumb ox, why didn't he just give me the keys?*

Mike said quietly: "So what do we do with Petey-O, chum?"

"Leave him alone."

"I want his gun," Mike said. "Get out of my way."

"I said, leave him alone!"

Mike looked at Johnny queerly. There was a funny smile on Mike's lips. He turned back to Pete and kicked him. His foot came back for another kick before Johnny smashed into him and drove him away savagely.

"Lay off him!"

Mike staggered, straightened. His eyes blazed. "I thought you hated his guts."

"You did enough to him, didn't you?"

"I hardly started. I want some fun with him."

Johnny knew there was something in Mike that was beyond words or reason. Stitch had been right. He was a creep. Mike would enjoy beating and stomping Pete to death, while Pete was helpless. Somehow, he couldn't let that happen. At the same time, he didn't know how to control Mike. All at once he reached over and took the keys dangling from Mike's fingers and muttered: "Let's get that door open." He turned away. "Comber's gonna bust a blood vessel if we don't step on it."

Mike hesitated, then shrugged and reluctantly retreated from Pete's contorted body. There was a wide hallway off Pete's office, scarred by iron skid wheels, with steel plates set here and there in the floor, as slippery as glass. The loading doors were at the far end of the corridor, where the passage opened into a huge, echoing storage room. There was no light down here. Johnny paused, wanting to return for the bull's-eye lantern Pete had dropped; but he didn't think it wise to draw Mike's attention back to Pete. He plunged on, hoping that Mike would follow closely.

The big doors yielded to the key he had taken from Pete. Johnny was shaking with impatience now. He felt alternately hot and sweaty, and then cold, as if he were coming down with a chill. But there was no turning back now, and he reminded himself of this as he heaved his weight against the roller door and pushed the huge, corrugated panel to one side. It made a clashing, grinding, grating noise that echoed thunderously through the huge storage room.

The hot night yawned beyond the doorway like the black maw of a waiting beast.

The loading ramp was dark.

Comber's truck and Comber's men were not there. Johnny swung around wildly. The storage room was filled with shadows, with crates stacked high to the ceiling. Which ones did Comber want? He didn't know. That was part of the job that Comber's men were supposed to take care of. But where were they?

He went out on the rough wooden platform and looked up and down the dark, deserted street. He saw no one. His throat went dry. His part of the job was done. The warehouse was cracked open. It had gone easily enough. But now the feeling came to him that something was desperately wrong.

He wasn't worried about Pete talking later. He knew that once the warehouse was cleaned out, Pete would keep his mouth shut. Pete wouldn't rat on his own brother. Besides, if he did, the blues wouldn't believe him; they'd think he was faking the story.

From a distance, Johnny heard the lonesome chuffing of a switch engine on the railroad spur nearby. A whistle hooted. On the hot night air, he heard, or imagined he heard, the sudden throb of a truck engine, moving away out of sight. But Comber's truck didn't come around the corner.

He wasn't ready for the explosive, racketing shot that came from behind him.

Mike yelled in alarm, and Johnny twisted, dropping to a half crouch, searching down the corridor by which they had entered the store-room. It was Pete. He was on his knees, a small figure in the faint gloom far, far back there. He held his service gun in both hands, pointing it this way.

Pointing it at Johnny, his brother.

The gun crashed again. The noise of it was like the world collapsing, bursting, falling down in shattered pieces.

Johnny ran. His one thought was to get away from the incredible picture of Pete, on his knees, in agony, pointing and firing that gun at him.

He didn't know where Mike went, and he didn't care. Panic took him and carried him along on a swift, destructive tidal wave that swept him over the platform, leaping in the street with arms wide, falling to his knees, scrambling up, and running for the darkness at the other end.

When he was halfway there he saw the patrol car slide around the corner and come to a halt, blocking his way. Jesus, what had gone wrong?

He skidded to a halt, twisted, ran the other way.

His breath sobbed, squeezed together in his throat, choked him. He didn't want to get caught. He thought fleetingly of Mike, that crazy, queer son of a bitch. But Mike had vanished into the shadows from which he had come. He had the feeling that Mike wasn't real, that Mike existed only in his imagination. Where had he gone?

He saw the narrow, weed-grown driveway behind the warehouse flanked on one side by the blank brick wall, on the other by the wire fence that marked the boundary of the railroad property. It was dark, inviting, a slot into which he could dart and hide. He turned and ran into it.

It was a mistake.

The railroad spur came around in a long, gentle curve between the industrial buildings on either side of the right-of-way. There was a signal bridge a little farther on, with red, yellow, and amber lights winking and sliding and shining on the ribbons of steel that came toward Johnny. And just passing under the signal bridge was the switch engine he had heard only a moment ago. It was coming his way, moving very slowly, but the ghastly, blazing eye of its head-light swept with implacable brilliance along the weedy driveway where Johnny tried to hide.

He jumped up, grabbing at the wire fence, tried to

find a toehold, and couldn't. The wire bit savagely into his hands and he had to let go. He dropped down into the weeds again. There was only the blank brick wall of the warehouse on this side. He had no place to go. And when he turned his head to look at the entrance he had used to get in here, he saw the shape of Sergeant Vallera running toward him.

He heard Vallera shout his name, but it was drowned out in the shrill hoot of the switch-engine. Johnny was still pinned in the bright glare of its headlight.

Panting, cursing, he turned and ran for the other end of the driveway.

He was almost there when someone else burst into view.

Johnny saw only the figure of a tall man with arms spread wide as if to catch him as he darted out of the alley to safety.

Nobody was going to stop him, he thought desperately.

He wouldn't get caught. He wouldn't!

"Johnny, wait ..." The man called.

Johnny crashed into him. He had the gun in his hand and the man grabbed for it, and Johnny smashed a fist into the man's face and scrambled away. The man held on to his ankle, to his dungaree cuff, and wouldn't let go.

"Johnny Broom ..."

"Let me go!" Johnny screamed.

He didn't know who it was.

All he knew was that he had to get away from Vallera, still a good distance away.

He raised the gun Comber had given him and fired it at the face of the man who tried to hold him here.

Only then, with the gun exploding in his hand, tearing the world apart with its noise, did he see it was Henry Dexter Stephens.

Chapter Eight

There was a stunned moment when time stood still for Johnny Broom.

He saw Stephens' face dissolve in a shattered mess of bone and flesh.

He knew Stephens was dead.

He knew he had shot and killed a man.

But his mind rejected it.

For another moment, Johnny stood panting over the dead man. His mind screamed at the body: *Why didn't you let me get away? Why'd you have to try to stop me?*

The dead man didn't answer. The dead man lay there in his fine sharkskin summer suit and the blood stopped running out of his head and just made a quiet pool of darkness under the sharp, thin profile of Henry Dexter Stephens.

Johnny's mind screamed silently at him: *Run, Johnny, run!*

He couldn't run. He couldn't breathe. The heat of the night crushed him, smashed him to the spot, held him paralyzed.

Vallera's pounding feet broke the spell. Johnny turned his head, panting, in a half crouch over the dead man, and looked that way. Vallera was halfway down the long driveway toward him. The switch-engine, still coming around the curve, had passed over Johnny with its bright, glaring eye of a headlight. The headlight shone straight into Vallera's angry, congested face. Suddenly Johnny knew that Vallera hadn't seen anything, *couldn't* have seen anything, with the blinding light in his eyes.

With the thought came a sudden release from the paralyzing panic that rooted him there.

He straightened up. He stepped on Stephens' leg and wasn't aware of it. And then he ran.

Later, he couldn't remember how he had come or the way he had chosen. The night held him for long, blank moments in its hot, pulsing palm. He ran and he walked and he ran again, and when his lungs burned and his heart threatened to burst, he walked again. He had no idea where Mike was. He didn't know what had happened to Pete or what Pete might be telling the cops. He didn't think about Henry Dexter Stephens. He tried to forget it. He put it out of his mind and counted the steps he took, fifty, and then he counted the steps he ran, fifty more, and then over and over again, while he put time and distance between himself and the warehouse.

It was a long time before he remembered Stitch and Flopsy in the car.

God, what a mess the night had turned into!

He knew now why Comber's truck hadn't followed him to the warehouse. They must have spotted Vallera's car. That son-of-a-bitch of a Vallera! It was his fault, Johnny thought. Too smart for his own good, tipped off about the rumble, and he hadn't been satisfied with that, no, he had to snoop farther, he had to follow him and Stitch to Frankford and Pete's warehouse. Too goddam smart, and it was Vallera's fault that Stephens had been killed.

For the first time he wondered why Stephens had been there at all.

It didn't make sense.

He knew Stephens by sight, he had even spoken to the man that time when Pete had insisted he at least visit the Neighborhood Club, which Stephens had sponsored, and give it a try.

Johnny figured that Stephens must have been with Vallera in the patrol car.

In that case, the whole thing never really had a chance. It was as if the plan had been broadcast all over town, and the only ones who hadn't known what was going to happen had been himself and Dumb-Ox-Pete.

His leg suddenly felt weak and trembly under him and he sat down on a brownstone step. He couldn't walk or run anymore. It was no good, anyway, just smashing around through the night, not knowing where to go or what to do or what was happening. He had to stop and figure things out. He had to decide what to do.

He still had the gun.

Somebody said to him, "What are you doing with that gun, white-boy?"

He turned his head and saw a tall, thin Negro woman in a flowered print dress on the top of the steps where he sat. She had come out of the house and stood looking down at him. The door was open behind her. Johnny lifted his head and saw for the first time that there were other people on the block, some walking along the sidewalk, some just sitting and suffering and sweltering in the heat of the night.

"What?" he said. "What did you say, lady?"

"I asked about that gun in your hand, white boy."

Her eyes told him she wasn't afraid of him. He wondered why she wasn't afraid. He said, "That's not a gun."

"It looks like one. You been running too. You shoot somebody, boy?"

"No," he said. "It's a toy."

"It ain't."

He looked at her. "Lady, it's a toy. I didn't shoot anybody."

The way he looked at her made her step back into the doorway. "All right, white boy, if you say so. Whatever you say."

She turned and went into the house. Johnny wondered if she had gone in to get her old man. He decided he'd better not stay here, even though he wasn't rested yet, and he got up and walked down the block and turned the corner.

Nobody followed him.

When he came to the first alley, he saw trash cans and he dropped the gun into one. Then he walked to the next corner and paused. He saw a cop standing and talking to a man outside a candy store. The cop didn't see him. Johnny turned and retraced his steps and found the trash can and retrieved the gun from it. He decided he'd better keep it. Nobody was going to catch him. Nobody, ever.

He didn't know when this decision had come to him, but he felt better for having made it.

He went farther into the alley and found another trash can and sat down on it and slowly bent over, his head in his hands, lowered to his knees. The gun jabbed angrily into his side from under his belt, but he didn't move it. He wanted to know it was still there. It was the only friend he had, at the moment.

He had to decide what to do.

In the darkness and the solitude, in the heat and the stench of the alley, he felt safe. But it wouldn't last for long. They would start looking for him soon. They'd look everywhere, and they wouldn't stop trying to find him.

For the first time, the true enormity of the murder touched him, along with the fact that he, Johnny Broom, had killed a man. And they would call him a murderer.

It was as if he had taken a last step down those

dark, endless stairs, and found it had an end, indeed—an end into nothingness. He felt as if he were falling, into a black eternity, and his stomach turned over and all at once he was sick, suddenly and violently, squatting there in the smells of the alley, vomiting on the wet, black concrete paving, vomiting until his lungs ached and his stomach felt as if he had been stomped on and his breath stank and burned in his throat.

When the sudden spasm was over, he felt better.

He even felt a little hungry.

But first he had to make sure that nobody would catch him. The cops would be out looking, hunting, poking and prying, searching him out. They'd come rolling silently in their patrol cars and turn the bright spotlights into every corner, every dark pocket, every slot of an alley....

He jumped up and got out of the alley and walked west and then south.

He needed help. He wanted to understand what had happened.

The only place he knew he could go for help was Comber's. Comber would help him, all right. Comber had put him up to this, and even though things had gone wrong, Comber would give him a lift, a hand up out of this mess. It would be all right, he thought hopefully, if he could get to Comber.

While he walked, Johnny pretended that things might be all right, too, if he went home. If he went upstairs to his room and stretched out on his bed and waited for Pete to get back from his night trick.

Only, Pete wouldn't be coming back so soon. Pete was probably in a hospital now, because of what that crazy Mike had done to him.

He wondered if Vallera had caught Mike. He didn't care. Then he did care, because Mike would probably squeal his head off about this caper. So then he hoped that Mike had gotten clean away.

Maybe Stitch and Flopsy had gotten away too. Sure, Johnny decided, they'd gone. Stitch would have heard the shots and gone chicken, crapped in his pants and high-tailed out of there. Why hadn't he even thought to try to get back to the wheels? He didn't know. He'd gone crazy with fright back there, after shooting Stephens. He'd just run the wrong way, that was all.

So Stitch and Flopsy and Mike had got away, there was only Pete left. And Vallera. But Vallera hadn't actually seen anything, had he? How could he, with that locomotive headlight shining in his eyes? Nobody could prove that Johnny had actually done the shooting.

And Pete wouldn't talk. Or would he? Johnny suddenly remembered the way Pete's face, no longer placid, or mildly worried, or puzzled over his crazy kid brother Johnny, had changed back there in the warehouse. It had turned into the hard, angry unyielding face of a stranger.

But Pete would hardly rat on his own brother.

Maybe, Johnny thought, panting with new hope, if things got in a real bad clutch, everything could be blamed on Mike. But nobody knew who Mike was.

Mike was just a thing in the night, a nameless shadow who drifted in and out of the neighborhood.

He moved with care now. First he stopped at a delicatessen and bought a sandwich and a bottle of coke, and he walked along the dark, hot streets, eating and drinking. His stomach felt better. He told himself it had been stupid to get sick like that; he'd never gotten sick before, not since he could remember. But he'd never been in a jam like this before, either.

It was past midnight when he reached the neighborhood of Comber's cigar store. Caution still walked with him, and he scouted the streets carefully for signs of any blue heat before he approached. He had been thinking about Comber. The fat man had promised him a couple of bills for the job, and even if the job had folded, he figured that Comber still owed him *something*. A hundred bucks would see him on his way. He could get out of town and hole up somewhere, maybe down along the shore, and relax and think things out. Maybe Comber would get some legal eagle to help. Things would work out. He could have a good time down in Atlantic City with a hundred. He'd find himself a cool pad and rest and maybe find a broad to help him pass the time until the heat was off.

He was feeling hopeful when he went into the cigar store.

Comber's hoods still loafed and loitered on the sidewalk. They looked as if they hadn't moved in all the hours since last Johnny had come here with Stitch.

Comber didn't look any different, either. Not at first. He stood behind the glass tobacco counter, his bald head shining in the queer brown light, his silk shirt dark with sweat stains, his eyes like moving spiders under his thick, straight brows.

Then Johnny saw the way the spider eyes looked at him, totally black and forbidding. He felt a moment of apprehension and grinned.

"Hi, Mr. Comber."

"That all you got to say? Hi?" Comber's voice was high and reedy. "You goddam, stupid punk kid, you come here and say hi?"

"Look, Mr. Comber, you know what happened, don't you?" Johnny said. He stammered a little, and hated himself for it. "I need some help, Mr. Comber.

I need help real bad—"

"Come with me," Comber said abruptly.

He came out from behind the glass cigar counter, tottering in the effort to balance his huge belly on his scrawny legs, into the familiar room upstairs in the rear. Comber's breath wheezed and whistled as he went through the doorway as if heading for his rolltop desk. But the next instant Johnny felt his shirt grabbed in a fat, massive hand and he was almost yanked off his feet as Comber fiercely dragged him toward him.

"You punk kid! You stupid little rat!" Comber's breath hissed with rage. "What did you come here for, hey? Why'd you bring the heat here?"

Johnny struggled to break free of the fat man's angry grip. He couldn't do it. He had never suspected Comber's enormous strength.

"I didn't, Mr. Comber," he gasped. "Nobody saw me come here, I swear it!"

"You swear it! You snotty brat, how do you know?"

"I was careful! I know I wasn't followed."

"The real heat's on you, you know that?" Comber shook him to punctuate his words. "You know what you done, you hopped-up brat? You know—"

"I didn't use anything, no pod, nothing, I swear!"

"Then why'd you shoot Stephens?"

"I had to. He was in my way. We had to get away, Mr. Comber, the blues were all around the place—"

"How come?"

"I don't know. I don't know. Let me go, Mr. Comber!"

"You hadda pick Stephens, hey? You hadda knock off the biggest name in town right now! Give you a gun, and you gotta use it on anybody you see, hey? Not your dumb brother. Oh, no! On Henry

Dexter Stephens!"

Johnny struggled again and tore from Comber's massive grip. His red shirt tore and the suddenness of his release sent him staggering to the couch. He fell down on it and wiggled around quickly, expecting a blow, but Comber stood where he was, breathing heavily, eyeing him with cold, implacable hatred.

"Wait here," Comber said.

"Sure, Mr. Comber. Whatever you say. I can explain—"

Comber didn't look at him as he went out. Johnny listened to his heavy tread on the stairs going down, and then he couldn't hear anything further. He sat up. His heart pounded, and he sweated. He told himself that Comber was just sore, like you get sore when you're relieved, and that Comber was really glad to find him and see that he wasn't caught by the blues. He told himself this and tried to believe it, but he couldn't. There was something too different about Comber. Johnny reached in his pocket, felt the bulk of the gun, and fumbled in the other pocket for a cigarette. His pack was crumpled, and there was only one cigarette left in it. He tried to light it, but his hands were shaking, and he had trouble getting the match going. He threw the cigarette and the matches to the floor and stood up in panic.

Suppose Comber was going to call the blues and turn him over to Vallera?

Comber might just do that. Comber might figure that was the smart way to make himself innocent for what had happened tonight. Play the part of a good citizen, turn him in, wash his hands of it all.

Johnny felt his heart pound crazily in his chest. He ran to the door and tried to open it.

The door was locked.

He hadn't heard Comber turn the key in it. The

fat bastard had been too sly for him. He was a prisoner already, in this room!

Turning, Johnny spun in a full, erratic circle, surveying the room. Why had Comber locked him in? To keep him for the blues? He looked around and saw the two single, tall windows in the back wall and he ran to them. The glass was painted black. He couldn't see out through the windows. He tried to raise one. It was nailed shut. He ran to the other window. It was fixed the same way. He couldn't get out unless he broke the glass. And even then, he was on the second floor, and it was too far down to jump.

The breath sobbed and burned in his throat. He sat down on the couch where Flopsy had happily burned pod only a half-dozen hours ago and wondered what he could do. He couldn't think of anything. He was trapped.

Then Comber came back.

Johnny looked quickly beyond him, expecting to see Vallera or some of Comber's muscle. But Comber was alone. He felt a great wave of relief and then a new squirm of nausea in his stomach. He swallowed it down and stood up.

"Mr. Comber, I just came here for help. I know you'll help me. I'm counting on it. It wasn't my fault the thing went wrong. I got the doors open, and the crates were right there, but the truck didn't show up. Why didn't your truck show up, Mr. Comber? It might have been all right if your men were there."

"You think so?" Comber asked quietly. He looked awkward, that massive body and huge, bulging belly on his pipestem legs. Johnny looked at the broad, brass-studded belt Comber wore and remembered the stories he'd heard about Comber's belt and of the way he could use it. He licked his lips.

"I don't know how the cops got there," Johnny

added feebly.

"They just followed you, stupid."

"But we were careful—"

"Not careful enough. My boys in the truck saw them and took off. They figured you'd have sense enough to do the same."

"We—we didn't see the blues," Johnny whispered.

"I guess you didn't." Comber sat down at the rolltop desk and studied Johnny malevolently. "How come Mr. Stephens was there?"

"I don't know, Mr. Comber."

"You know he's dead, don't you?"

"I didn't stay around to see," Johnny muttered. "Please, Mr. Comber, you know I'm in bad trouble. You're going to help me, aren't you?"

"Where are your friends? The girl, Flopsy, and Stitch?"

"I don't know."

"What *do* you know, stupid?"

Johnny didn't answer. He kneaded his hands together. It wasn't going with Mr. Comber the way he had hoped and expected. He didn't understand the way Comber was acting. Like a cop, giving him the third degree or something. It didn't make sense.

Comber breathed in and out like a fish with his mouth open. His voice changed. It was quieter. "You know that killing a man like Stephens is going to bring a lot of heat, don't you?"

"Yeah," Johnny muttered.

"You used the gun I gave you on him?"

"Yes."

"Still got it?"

"Yes."

"Let's have it," Comber said, holding out a fishy-white hand, palm up, toward Johnny.

Johnny stared at him. "But I may need it, Mr.

Comber."

"You're not going to shoot anybody else, boy."

"But the blues—"

"Give me the gun, boy."

Johnny stood up. He took out the gun, but he didn't give it to Comber. He saw the spiders move in the fat man's eyes, glinting black with hatred. And something else he saw. Fear. Comber afraid of him! Johnny suddenly saw this as a great burst of revelation. Comber feared him while he still had the gun.

"Will you help me, Mr. Comber," he asked.

"What do you want?"

He didn't hesitate. "A couple of notes. Two hundred will do. I figure that can get me out of town, maybe down to the shore, and I can hole up while you get the heat off me."

"While I get the—" Comber started to rise from the chair, then sat down, eyeing the gun in Johnny's hand. He breathed wheezily. "You must be out of your mind."

"You can do it, Mr. Comber," Johnny said urgently.

"Some heat I can cool, sure. I could find you a cool pad for some things you might do. But you don't know how big this is, do you? *You killed Henry Dexter Stephens!*"

"I know, but—"

"You killed the guy they called the best friend you kids ever had!"

"That's a lot of crap!"

"People in this city believe it. The heat is going to burn you, boy. You'll never make it out of town."

"I can try."

"And get caught. And spill your guts about Comber to the blues, is that it, hey?"

Now, Johnny thought, now he had it. Now he'd reached the root of Comber's fear and hatred of him.

He said quietly: "I wouldn't talk, Mr. Comber, no matter what they did to me. You can count on that."

"Nuts!" Comber said quietly. "You'd spill your guts all over the place, the minute you saw Vallera comin' at you."

Johnny didn't deny it. His head felt suddenly clear and icy-cold. His thoughts moved steadily down, slowly and quietly, like the flakes of a snowfall.

"Give me the gun, Johnny," Comber said. "I'll take care of you right here."

"I thought you didn't want me around here," Johnny said,

"I'll do what I can for you. Give me the rod."

"Suppose I don't?" Johnny said, and laughed.

"What?" Comber stared at him. "What's that?"

"Suppose I keep the gun?"

Comber said flatly, "You threatening me with it?"

"Maybe."

"You holding me up for dough?"

"It's an idea. Right? Hey, Comber?" Johnny dropped the Mister deliberately. "It kinda jolts you, doesn't it? Hey, Comber? I killed Stephens, and I can't get hurt more for it if I kill anybody else with this gun you gave me." He felt a sudden thrill in the way Comber recoiled from his words. A tremendous feeling of power surged up in him, an excitement that burned and tingled in his fingertips. "How much money you got in that old desk of yours, Comber? As much as I'll need?"

"You don't get out of here alive, boy," Comber hissed. He shook his bald head, and the huge, drooping wattles on his jaw flapped one way and then the other. "I'm glad you came back here, boy. I was worried the blues might get you and make you spill. But you came home to Comber, didn't you? So now I can take care of you, like I'll take care of your punk friends who were with you. That Stitch and Flopsy, they don't know nothin'. I'm not much worried about them. But I was worried about you, boy, and the gun I gave you."

"You're still worried about it," Johnny said.

"Not anymore. Now I see the punk you are. My boys are waitin' downstairs in the store. They don't let you out, punk. You stay here. Maybe you stay here forever, hey?"

"Get up," Johnny said.

Comber didn't move.

Johnny walked over to him, with the gun in his hand, and when Comber remained seated in the swivel chair, Johnny suddenly hit him in the side of the head with the gun, raking his bald scalp with the muzzle, and Comber fell out of the chair with a sudden, astonished grunt and crashed ponderously to the floor. Johnny ripped open the old-fashioned roll top on the desk and looked inside. There was nothing but papers in the pigeon-holes. He yanked open one drawer, then another. More papers. He threw them wildly aside, hungry now, impatient, looking for money. He searched all through the big desk, but there was no money.

Comber was crawling on the floor toward the door. He looked ludicrous, no longer an object of terror and power; he dragged his belly and his flat flanks and skinny legs looked helpless and weak; his big, bald head was bleeding. Johnny walked around him and stood in front of him, the gun dangling from his fingers.

"Where is your money?"

"My wife," Comber gasped. "My wife keeps it all."

"You're lying!"

"No, no. Johnny-O, please—use your head, don't do anything crazy."

"I won't. I'm getting out of here. You get your muscle out of my way, hear? Nobody's going to stop me. I thought I could count on you for help," Johnny said harshly, "but I see you'd just drop me in the river to shut my mouth. I told you I'd never rat to the blues, but you didn't believe me. Now it's too late. I can't trust you, Comber. I ain't got a friend in the world now. That makes it easier, see? No friends, you don't have to worry who's your enemy, because everybody's my enemy now. Understand that, Comber?"

"Help me up, Johnny," Comber whispered.

"Help yourself."

"Damn you—"

Comber raised himself to a kneeling position. His huge paunch hung down between his bony knees. He was gasping for breath and the blood on his scalp ran down one side of his face in little, wriggly, dark lines. He clawed for the edge of the couch, missed and fell over on his side again, gasping. Johnny watched impassively, not touching the fat man. Finally Comber got a grip on the couch and pulled himself up on it like a huge slug and sat down, gasping, holding his belly, his face purplish, his eyes crawling under his thick black brows.

"On your feet," Johnny said. "Walk me out of here."

"I can't—"

"You said your hoods were waiting for me."

"I was only joking, Johnny—"

"Get up," Johnny said.

Comber got up. They walked down the narrow back stairs together and entered the cigar store by the back door. Three of Comber's boys were standing there, looking uncertain.

Comber said heavily, "Let the punk go."

One of the hoods said, "But you told us—"

"Let him go." He added viciously, "We'll take care of him later."

Chapter Nine

Johnny moved by way of alleys and narrow side streets toward the Lancers' headquarters. He didn't know where else to go. There was thunder in the sky, dark and heavy, and the night air was just as hot as before, maybe hotter, with that quiet, electric feeling that comes before a storm. Every smell in every alley and house was heightened and accented by the oppressive air.

Every man was against him.

For a few minutes after escaping from Comber, he had wandered aimlessly, not knowing which way to turn or what to do. He needed money. He didn't dare go home and raid Pete's pants pockets. He knew Pete kept a few bills in the kitchen sugar bowl, but it was too risky to go back there. Vallera might expect him to act like a kid and run home and hide in bed; so he wouldn't do the expected. He needed money and he needed wheels, and he decided the best thing to do was to find Stitch Pollard and Flopsy and get the car.

He went to the auto graveyard first, pushed open the gate they had left unlocked, and drifted among the wrecked bulks of rusting sedans and truck bodies until he came to the niche where he and Stitch secreted the Pontiac.

His relief was so enormous that he almost fell to his knees.

The car was here.

It was a sign that Stitch and Flopsy had escaped from the blues and had gotten clean away.

Johnny went over to the car and felt the hood. The engine was still slightly warm. He looked inside, called Stitch's name softly, but Stitch and Flopsy weren't here. That didn't matter. The keys were gone, too, but it would be a simple matter to jump the wires. Then he wondered how much gas there was in the tank. He remembered there hadn't been too much. Well, he could siphon some out of somebody's parked car. Or better yet, he could use the gun on some crummy passerby and lift the dough to buy some.

No, that was no good.

He didn't want to give Vallera the slightest clue as to where he might be.

Then he knew the Pontiac wouldn't be much good, either, because if Vallera had tailed him from Sandor's Bowling Alley to the warehouse, then Vallera knew damned well about the car and its description was probably broadcast over three states by now.

No, the car was too hot to use.

Why hadn't he thought of it before bothering to come over here? Johnny felt annoyed at himself. The gun wouldn't be enough to keep his freedom. You had to be smart; you had to use your head to stay clear of the law. Stay cool, and you could accomplish anything.

He walked from there to the Lancers' headquarters.

Twice he had to dodge back into the shadows because of ghostly sliding patrol cars that drifted by, and the second time it was just by the skin of his teeth that he ducked into the wreckage of an abandoned row-house and avoided the problem of the probing spotlight beam that looked for him.

It was almost two o'clock before he lowered himself into the cellar window and dropped into the empty coal bin of the house shell where the Lancers met before.

He waited in the darkness of the cellar—waited and listened. He didn't hear anything. There was nothing to alarm him. So he went forward and pushed open the wooden door in the partition that divided the cellar and entered the room where he had beaten down the Judge's rebellion.

The Judge was still there.

The albino looked like a pale, unnatural statue, sitting on a stool by the light of a single candle stuck in its wax on the dusty cellar floor. Nobody else was around. Jennings looked up at him with pale, blind eyes and laughed.

"Welcome back to the morgue, big shot."

Johnny leaned back against the wooden partition. "Where is everybody?"

"Dead."

"Come on, where are they?"

"You ought to know, Johnny. You walked them into the trap. You crossed us all up, didn't you?"

"Look, you don't understand—"

"We understand, man. We know the kind of rat you are."

"Were you at Sandor's?" Johnny asked.

"No, but a couple of the guys got away and told me about it. The rat-trap you led them into! Bad enough the Violets knew we were coming. Bad enough the blues were waiting too. But then you chicken out; you run away and go off on business of your own." The Judge's voice was flat and empty of emotion. He still showed the marks of the beating

Johnny had given him. "How does it feel, Johnny?"

"I don't know what you're talking about," Johnny said lamely.

"How does it feel to be a killer?"

Johnny said tightly, "How do you know about that?"

"It's on the radio. Didn't you listen? You're a big shot, killer. You ought to listen. Your name is on every station in town. You and Henry Dexter Stephens. You do things big, don't you, killer, when you decide to be a rat."

"Shut up," Johnny said. "Shut up, you hear?"

"What'll you do, kill me, too, if I don't button the lip?"

Johnny didn't know what to say. It was strange that the Judge wasn't afraid of him anymore. The Judge had been badly beaten and cowed before the rumble. But now he was different. Different like Comber had been. He wondered what was happening to everybody. He didn't understand it.

Johnny sat down on the cellar floor and leaned his shoulders against the wooden partition and fumbled in his pocket for a smoke. When he looked up, the Judge was standing and offering him a Camel.

"The condemned man gets a butt at least, before they burn him," the albino said.

Johnny took the cigarette. "What are you talking about? They haven't caught me yet—and they won't, either. Not ever."

"You're dragging yourself, Johnny-O. You can't last, man."

Johnny felt tired. He felt as if he had been running forever through this hot, endless night. His trousers felt sticky with sweat all the way from his flat stomach and groin, down his legs. It was good to sit down for a while. He lit the cigarette and exhaled gratefully.

"Have you seen Stitch and Flopsy?" he asked the Judge.

"Not me. But a couple of the guys—those who ain't in the can or the hospital—they saw 'em. They're around. Running scared." The Judge sat down again. The flickering candle sputtered and made strange shadows on the albino's face and cropped white hair. "I'm surprised you danced in here, man. You ought to keep running."

"I'm safe here," Johnny said.

"You think so? You're lucky I'm alone."

"What does that mean?"

"We're going to get you, man, if the blues don't get you first. You think we'll let you get away with crossing the Lancers? You think we just forget the way you ratted and sold us out, so you could do a job for Comber and suck up to that fat slob?"

"Comber and me are on the outs," Johnny muttered.

The Judge laughed. "What did you expect, like? He'd kiss you? He'll kiss you off, like we already done."

Johnny jumped up. "I'm not afraid of any of you jerks. You can't touch me. I won't be around long, anyway."

"That's for sure," the Judge said.

Johnny went out of the clubroom the way he had come in. There was no point in hanging around there, just asking for trouble. He had trouble enough. He was only beginning now to see the depth and dimensions of it.

He felt trapped by the night and the city that pressed in all around him. He was alone. There was nobody he could turn to. He thought of Comber, that fat slug. All Comber cared about was his own ugly skin. All he worried about was whether Johnny would talk about the warehouse plan and where he got the gun, if the blues grabbed him. Well, he'd talk plenty, if it came to that, he decided sullenly. Only, nobody was going to catch him. Not tonight, or ever.

He thought of the Judge, the way the albino sat there in the cellar like some animal in a burrow. He hadn't expected much from the Lancers, anyway, Johnny told himself. A bunch of jerks, too dumb to know which end was up. So he had crossed them— but he hadn't meant for anything bad to happen to the guys. He hadn't meant for Comber to tip the blues and the Violets about the rumble. It was Comber's fault, not his. If Comber hadn't tipped the cops, then it would've been just a rumble, nothing special, done and over with. And nobody would have known about the warehouse thing at all.

And now Comber's boys were looking for him.

And the Lancers, goaded by the Judge, would be merciless.

And the cops—

Johnny shivered. He felt more alone than ever. He hadn't meant to kill Stephens. He hadn't even known who the man was, until after the shot was fired. He hadn't even meant to use the gun at all.

But he had. And Stephens was dead.

How had it happened? How did it begin?

For several minutes he sat on a brownstone step, wishing fervently he could go back in time, back to the hour when he lay on the roof coping and Pete was heckling him about taking a job in the warehouse.

Why hadn't Pete understood what he really wanted? Nobody ever listened to you in this world, Johnny thought. You couldn't talk to a person and expect them really to hear what you were saying.

Nobody cared, that was the trouble.

Nobody gave the smallest damn about you.

But they cared now. Now the name of Johnny Broom was broadcast all over the city.

Once he would have relished the thought of being so important. But now that it had happened, he only felt frightened. He wanted to hide, to become nothing and nobody again.

He had joined the Lancers because of a need to belong somewhere. Pete was all right, but Pete worked always at night, and he slept most of the day. And Pete was much older, so there was no understanding between them as brothers.

The Lancers gave Johnny a chance to feel important in a world that was too preoccupied to notice Johnny Broom. There was a time when he had been interested in school too.

He'd been good in math, even in algebra and the half-year of trig they gave you. But it was too easy for him, and the class went much too slowly, trying to drag the dumb-heads along with the course. Mr. Kessler, who taught math, hadn't understood Johnny's sudden failing of interest. It was because Johnny wanted to go on and learn more than the slow-moving class had to offer; and because he couldn't, because old Kessler had enough on his hands trying to keep the joint disciplined and pass as many of the dumb-heads as possible, Johnny knew he was ignored.

He turned to shop work next, and for a time he thought he'd found the answer to his restlessness. There was a mathematical precision in machine tools that appealed to him. But the equipment was often broken, often vandalized by the guys, and it took forever before you had a chance at the lathes and presses. By the time you got to it, you didn't care whether you finished your project or not.

He had talked to Lew McGee about it once. Lew was all right, even for a cop. Lew was younger than Pete, closer to Johnny—and at least, he listened.

"How do you figure you can go to a technical college, Johnny?" Lew had asked.

"I don't know. I don't know anything about it."

"But that's what you'd like to do, right?"

"Sure. I'd like that."

"Can't Pete help you with the money you need?"

"Pete?" Johnny laughed sourly. "Nah. He wants me to work with him in the old warehouse. Thinks college is too good for me." Johnny hadn't looked at Lew, but he knew Lew was watching him with some concern, and that was unusual enough to make him keep talking. "If there was any chance for a scholarship, Mr. McGee, I'd work like a dog to get it."

"Isn't there?"

"I asked Kessler, and I even went to old man Freedley, the principal. But they just brushed me off."

"Do you know why?"

Johnny shrugged. "I guess I just raised too much hell in class a few years ago. They don't figure I've grown up some since then. They got me down as a regular trouble-maker, and they don't want to change their minds?"

"*Were* you a trouble-maker, Johnny?"

He was truthful. "Yeah, I guess I was."

"And now?"

"I guess I still am. I can't seem to help it. I get bored, or something, I guess."

Lew had promised to see what he could do about getting Johnny into a technical school of some kind. But that was the last anybody ever heard of it. Lew kept saying he was working on it and maybe he actually tried, but Johnny knew, after six months went by, that nothing would come of it, and he didn't have a chance.

There didn't seem to be a chance for him anywhere.

And so he had turned back to the Jungle—to the things that first the Lancers promised to bring him, and then to the more tangible rewards of working for Comber....

He was passing an alley when he heard his name called. The voice came whispering out of the dark, and at first Johnny wasn't sure he'd heard it. He didn't even know where he was, for a moment. He had been wandering aimlessly, and now he saw that, consciously or not, he had drifted back into dangerous territory, close to home. He was on Tenth Street, only a block west from where Flopsy lived.

"Johnny!"

Mike came out of the shadows of the alley.

Johnny stared at him. "Where'd you come from?"

"Man, you shouldn't be dream-walking like that!" Mike said harshly. "What's the matter, you got rocks in your head?"

"How did you get away?" Johnny demanded.

"Come in here, man. We can't talk here."

"What about Stitch and Flopsy?"

"We got a pad in her backyard. Come on."

Johnny followed Mike's slight, lithe figure up the alley, between the leaning board fences. Cats hissed and spit and scrambled out of their way. Most of the houses were dark now, although a man was yelling and cursing in one of the back rooms they passed, and then a bottle broke up there. It made Johnny suddenly wish for a drink. He didn't often use liquor, but he had a sudden and powerful thirst for some, all at once.

Mike opened the wooden door in the fence, and he followed Johnny into Flopsy's backyard. Flopsy's people were unknown to Johnny. He had never been asked into her house, and he hadn't been interested enough to have any curiosity about her family. Nor did Flopsy ever talk about her folks in any way that made sense.

Stitch and the girl were sitting on a wooden bench—stolen from a public park, it looked like—in the tiny, fenced-in enclosure. The backyard had once been cemented, but the concrete had heaved and cracked, and there was only a broken jumble of paving and dirt and splintered packing cases. There was a wooden shed used as a summer kitchen attached to the back of the row house, but the rooms beyond were dark and nobody else was in sight.

Johnny became aware of an excitement in Mike that almost amounted to glee. He sat down beside Flopsy and immediately smelled more pod, and he wondered where she had gotten the new marijuana supply.

"Hey, killer," she giggled and tried to kiss him.

Johnny shoved her away. "Why didn't you wait in the car for me?"

Stitch spoke, stammering. "There was too much heat there, man. We had to wheel it away."

"So you just left me there," Johnny said bitterly. "I ought to clobber you."

"We had to, Johnny. We heard the shots, and Flopsy got scared." Stitch's round, moon face was earnest and frightened. "You know I wouldn't have ditched you if I could help it."

"Don't blame it on me, you stinky bastard," Flopsy said.

Johnny turned to Mike. They all spoke in low whispers, huddled in the darkness under the wooden fence. "What about you? What happened to you?"

"You got too panicky, Johnny. You should've waited."

"What for?" Johnny demanded.

Mike's face was wolfish in the shadows. "I went back to get your brother's gun."

"You're lying. He shot at us."

"He shot at *you*. He didn't see me until I got to him."

Johnny felt a sudden clutch of apprehension. "What did you do to him?"

"Nothing, Johnny."

"You're lying." Johnny suddenly jumped up and made a grab for Mike. He wanted to smash that superior, sardonic, vicious face. But Mike was faster than he. He was as elusive as a shadow, out of his grip before he could close with him. And Mike's voice was strangely cold. "Don't touch me, Johnny."

"If you went back and hurt Pete again—"

"There wasn't time. I didn't even get his gun, anyway. Get away from me, Johnny."

Johnny looked at Mike. Mike was half a head shorter and lighter, and yet something in the other boy's face made him halt. His anger ebbed and was replaced by something else. He wasn't sure what he felt toward Mike. Mike was too strange to be tagged easily. But he dropped his hands to his sides and sat down again beside Flopsy. Stitch giggled nervously.

"You're jumpy, Johnny. Relax, hey, man?"

Johnny laughed bitterly. How could he relax? Comber's men, the Lancers, the cops—everybody in town was out hunting for him.

"I got out the front door, Johnny," Mike said, in explanation. "The cops went around into that driveway, looking for you. They heard you roll those big loading doors open, I guess. So there was nothing in my way. I just walked out. But I heard your shot."

"You know what I did?" Johnny asked. "Do you know?"

"We know," Mike said. "We heard it on a radio."

"And I've still got the gun," Johnny said.

Mike spoke with soft eagerness.

"The question is, Johnny, what are you going to do with it?"

Chapter Ten

Rose Vallera awoke from a sleep that was not quite sleep and not quite waking. She sat up suddenly and felt her heart pound erratically. It was hot and dark in the front bedroom. She hadn't undressed completely, and she had stretched out in the room with the curved turret windows, wearing pants and bra. She was soaked with perspiration, and her body felt chilled.

She did not know what had wakened her until she looked at the clock beside the bed. It was ten minutes after two.

Usually, at two, Tom managed to bring the patrol car around to the house and slipped inside for a nip of rum in the kitchen, while Lew took a cup of coffee from the pot she always left for him. They were always quiet, and they rarely wakened her when they entered the house like that.

This time, she realized, she had awakened because they had *not* made their usual stop.

At first she wasn't sure, and she sat on the edge of the bed, shivering a little, and listened for the small reassuring noises the two men usually made down in the kitchen.

There was nothing.

The house held a forbidding emptiness.

Tomorrow was Sunday, and she didn't have to go to work, and it was Lew's day off too. She also remembered that Lew usually telephoned when he knew she'd be up late typing his lecture notes. He hadn't phoned tonight, and this somehow added to her feeling of alarm.

She got up and let her bra and pants slip to the floor, put on a thin robe and pulled the belt tight about her slim waist. The heat felt stupefying, and she went into the bath and splashed cold water on her cheeks and then she looked at the reflection of her oval face in the bathroom mirror and saw terror crawling in her eyes.

She didn't know what she was afraid of.

Once in a while something turned up during a duty tour that kept Tom and Lew from making their usual stop. She told herself it couldn't be anything important; she was being silly, made nervous by the tension of the heat, the thunderstorm that rolled and muttered around the horizons of the city and refused to break. She ought to go back to bed, she decided. But now, with the cold water on her face, she wasn't sleepy anymore.

Rose went downstairs. She didn't have to turn on any lights, because the corner lamppost shone blandly through the windows on the two exposed sides of the house and shed a pale yellow gloom in the big Victorian rooms. The front room, with its mahogany interior shutters, seemed brighter than usual, however, and she walked to the bowed front windows and looked out on the street.

Lights shone in the Broom house, midway down the block. She started to turn away, then remembered that Pete Broom had a night watchman's job and was never at home at this hour. Maybe it was young

Johnny, she thought. Then she saw the two cars parked at the curb, and the small knot of men on the steps. Something had happened over there. Two of the men were helping another into the house, and she saw by the light from the open front door that the one they were helping was Pete.

She knew Pete fairly well, having been brought up on the street together. She wondered if she should telephone to see if there was anything she could do. Probably there had been an accident. Then she realized it was none of her business and calling Pete might only be interpreted as interference.

She returned to the kitchen. The typewriter and Lew's lecture notes were still on the porcelain-topped table. She felt restless and considered typing some more, since it was impossible to sleep, and in less than two hours, their eight-hour tour of duty would be over anyway. She could have some coffee ready for Tom and Lew.

And talk to Tom.

Talk it out, about herself and Lew, once and for all.

And if that didn't resolve anything, at least she would insist finally on giving up this gloomy old corner house and finding a nice little apartment for Tom and herself.

Living in this house cluttered with Tom's painful memories was what might be driving him more and more desperately to the bottle.

She couldn't stand it anymore. Something had to change, because life had become an intolerable, depressing drift through days and weeks and months of frustration.

Rose unlocked the back kitchen door and stepped into the fenced backyard. The Vallera yard was larger than the others of the row houses beyond, since it was on the corner, but it was not as sheltered as the rest because of the hairpin wire fence on the street side. On the back, against the wooden fence there, was the huge old rose bush that bloomed only in June. It had been her mother's favorite, Rose thought; but it was ailing now, perhaps dying because of the stifling city air.

Something stirred in the dark corner shadows of the yard, and her heart suddenly leaped in irrational panic. But it was only a stalking cat, a creature of the night.

She went back into the house and returned to the front room to watch what was happening at the Broom place down the street.

She didn't realize she had forgotten to lock the back door.

At two-fifteen, nothing had been decided, and Mike Tarrant grew impatient. This night, which had built up into a roaring tidal wave of excitement, now threatened to taper off into aimless and uncertain waiting. He didn't want that. He wanted the excitement to continue. He fed on it and grew alive when danger pressed him. He didn't want it to end like this, huddled in Flopsy's back yard.

His mind jumped this way and that, toying with several ideas at once, seeking the peaks he had touched before. Just sitting here was no good. Flopsy and Stitch were sharing a stick of pod, murmuring and giggling to themselves. Johnny sat alone, hunched over in a foetal position, as if trying to retreat from a reality he had created. Only he, Mike, was alert and thinking.

Of course, he could slip away from these crums easily enough. He knew that Johnny was bound to be caught. And there were only three or four hours left before daylight, and he'd have to get home to Society Hill. Mike was reluctant to have things end like this, in static despair.

He considered just walking out on them. Johnny wouldn't try to stop him. Maybe he could get the gun away from Johnny and force him to turn himself in. That would be amusing; but he didn't see how he could do it without exposing himself. Maybe he could tip off the blues where to find Johnny. If he could watch what happened then, that would be fun. He looked around the area, seeking a place where he might return and spy on Johnny's final acts, if he called the cops. But he was disappointed to find no place of safety where he could hide as an observer. So that was out, too.

Anyway, he wanted more than just watching the night out.

He wanted to manipulate things so as to stretch out the excitement, bringing it to unbearable tension, so when he went home he would be sated and exhausted from it.

"Johnny, you asleep?" he whispered.

Johnny lifted his blond head. "No."

"You thinking of what to do next?"

"I can't think of anything."

"You've got to be scientific, man," Mike said. "Think of what you need. A car the cops don't know about, to get you out of town. Some dough to carry you. A cool pad where you can hide."

"I'm tired," Johnny said.

"I don't dig you," Mike insisted. "Man, are you just going to give up? They'll burn you, you know that? But you done us all a favor, getting rid of that stupid Stephens creep. We want to help you." Mike hugged the idea of Stephens being dead, killed in something that involved himself. He would enjoy breakfast that morning, with his father, Dr. Tarrant, reading the newspapers, seeing the big, black, inevitable headlines. And his mother, pale and shocked, saying: "Why, just last evening, Henry and Louise were *right here....*"

Mike could hardly wait for that scene. In some ways, that was the best part of it, watching his father and mother read the news of crime in the night, perhaps whispering to protect him, as they thought, from the sordid underworld, while he sat there, bland and polite, sipping orange juice served by Jane, with everything in him about what he really knew of the phony newspaper stories. Hugging the knowledge to yourself gave you a secret sense of power and superiority that was wonderful. Yes, sometimes he thought that was the very best part of it all.

Mike nudged into Johnny's torpor again. "You going to stay here all night? Can you use Flopsy's place to hide out in tomorrow?"

Flopsy pushed Stitch aside. "No, goddam it, I got two working sisters." She giggled. "They wouldn't leave poor Johnny alone."

Mike turned to look at her. "What do your sisters work at?"

"You know," Flopsy shrugged.

"What about you?" Mike asked. "You in the business, too?"

Flopsy stirred in anger. "Listen, you creep, no cracks outa you! Where do you dig this deal, anyway? I don't know you. You ain't a Lancer, you're just a nobody!"

"That's right," Mike said. He hated her. "A nobody."

"So what are you hanging around for? You're just a drag, man. Nobody needs you."

"I think Johnny needs me," Mike said.

"Yeah? What can you do for him?"

"I'll think of something," Mike said.

He had the beginning of an idea. It was the best idea he'd ever had. Absolutely the living end.

And a dead end for Johnny.

At two-thirty, Vallera and McGee were being questioned in the Precinct House. Two electric fans behind Deputy Commissioner Stanley and Captain Nolls, of Homicide, failed to relieve the close heat in the office. Somewhere in the back detention cells, a drunk wailed and sang in a monotonous, off-key chant. There was a smell of disinfectant, urine, sweat and woe in the room. There was a smell of tension, worry, recrimination and anger in the two big men facing Vallera and Lew McGee.

"I still don't understand how it happened, Vallera," Commissioner Stanley said. He looked as if he wished he were back in bed, asleep, at this hour of the morning. He was a florid man with unhealthy liver spots on hands and jowls. "We've got to get things straight for the newspapers, if nothing else. The story we gave out will hold them for a while, but not in the morning. How you could have let a man like Henry Dexter Stephens get into such a position of danger and be killed by some young hoodlum—"

"He got permission to ride with us from your office, Commissioner," Vallera said sullenly. "And he disobeyed my orders. He jumped out of the patrol car with the mistaken idea that he could stop the attempted robbery by reasoning with the punks."

"You're sure it was Johnny Broom who shot him?" Captain Nolls, of Homicide, asked.

"Yes, sir."

"You trailed Broom and his juvenile friends to the warehouse where his brother was employed, after seeing them leave the scene of the gang fight?"

"Yes, sir. I just had a hunch, sir."

"A hunch?"

"This Johnny Broom was always a bad one, sir. I've kept an eye on him for some time. He was bound to get into serious trouble."

Stanley muttered heavily, "He couldn't have chosen a worse victim. Damn it, I don't want the responsibility. The D.A. is in Atlantic City for the weekend. We're trying to locate him now."

Lew McGee stood at uneasy attention while Valera answered for them both. Now he spoke up. "Excuse me, Captain Nolls, but did Pete Broom identify his brother as one of the boys who invaded the warehouse?"

"No," Nolls said bluntly. "That's what troubles me."

"It's to be expected," Stanley complained. "He wouldn't finger his kid brother."

"Did he identify the other boy?" Lew persisted. "The one he says beat him up?"

"He described him."

Vallera said, "It has to be that Stitch Pollard punk."

"No, Pete Broom said this boy was small and dark and good-looking. He said he was different from Johnny's usual friends. He said he'd never seen him before, and Johnny called him by name. Mike."

Nolls said angrily, mopping sweat on his face: "Vallera, where would Johnny Broom have gotten that gun?"

"I don't know, sir."

"No idea of his source of supply?"

"No, sir. But if you let us go back on patrol, sir, I can find him. We'll get the truth out of the little bastard."

Stanley hesitated. "I don't know. The D.A. will want to talk to you two men down at the Hall, as soon as he gets back to town."

"That won't be for a couple of hours yet," Vallera insisted. "You can notify McGee and me when you want us by radio."

Nolls nodded. "You know the neighborhood, and you know these boys. You men understand, however, you're both in serious trouble. There's going to be a departmental investigation of this affair." He studied Vallera's stocky form meaningfully. "You've got a fine record, Tom. I'd hate to see it spoiled by what happened tonight."

Vallera said nothing. His face seemed carved of stone.

Lew McGee came down the steps from the Precinct House and rejoined Vallera in the patrol car parked at the curb. Vallera sat hunched over, as if he were ill, or exhausted. As Lew slid behind the wheel, he was immediately aware of the smell of fresh liquor on Vallera's breath, and he was startled by the risk Vallera took, hiding a bottle under the seat of the car.

He did not start the car immediately. "Are you all right, Tom?"

Vallera moved slightly. "Yeah, sure."

"How much did you take?"

"Just a mouthful or two. I needed it."

"You're a fool," Lew said quietly. Their animosity was forgotten now. Henry Dexter Stephens' death was too explosive, and the echoes and out-going waves of recrimination and charges were only just beginning. "You're going to have to face the D.A. soon enough."

"Shut up and let me think," Vallera muttered.

"But we're in this together," Lew insisted. "It's

not our fault Stephens jumped out of the car and got in the way. But we've got to stick together or we're both in a jam. You know that, don't you?" Lew drew a deep breath. "They'll say we were careless, and they'll charge you with taking too much on your own shoulders, knowing about the rumble and falling for Comber's phony tip—"

"I didn't fall for it," Vallera sighed. "I got to the warehouse, didn't I? We stopped the robbery."

"And Stephens, just the most important man in town, stopped a bullet," Lew said. "You were right there, but you can't identify the boy."

"It was Johnny Broom," Vallera said.

"You and I know you didn't see him. I was at the entrance to the driveway. That locomotive light blinded you."

Vallera lifted his shaggy head. "You didn't mention that, did you, McGee?"

"No."

"So the alarm is still out for Johnny Broom." Vallera lifted a big hand and dropped it heavily on his knee. "A thousand cops looking for that punk, but we've got to find him first, McGee. We've got to get that crazy kid before anybody else picks him up."

"And finds out your positive identification is false, is that it?" Lew asked flatly. "Suppose he isn't the right boy?"

"I know he is."

"I think so, too. But suppose we're wrong?" Lew insisted.

"He won't live to talk about it," Vallera said thinly.

Lew felt anger lift in him. "You can't just shoot him down! What's the matter with you, Tom? Being a cop doesn't make you infallible. Cops make mistakes too. Our job is to find the kid and bring him in for questioning—not kill him like a wild animal."

"But that's all he is." Vallera's voice grew stronger and he waved a hand for Lew to start the patrol car. "I've been on the Force for almost thirty years, McGee. Next year I get my pension, and I figure to buy Rose what she wants—a little apartment for the two of us, a decent place to live, out of the Jungle. I've got a good record, with four citations. You're still wet behind the ears, McGee—you don't know what life can do to you—what lettin' Stephens get killed can do to *me*. It's the finish of my whole life. And for Rose, too."

"And Johnny Broom," Lew pointed out.

Vallera wouldn't talk about it anymore. His mind was made up. He knew what had to be done.

"Let's find him," he said.

There were several points of reference Vallera used. He knew the Jungle better than any man on the Force, and his intimacy with the ways of the people here surpassed Lew McGee's by far.

They went to the Pollard house on 6th Street first, since Vallera knew that Stitch was Johnny's inseparable shadow. Vallera went in alone, ordering Lew to remain in the car. Vallera's manner with the Pollards was brutal and direct, waking them roughly from sound sleep, demanding Stitch's whereabouts. George Pollard, Stitch's father, was a mill-worker in Kensington. He was a thick-set, slow-spoken man with dull eyes and an Old World respect and fear for the law. But Vallera's blunt approach only confused him. A search was made of the house, waking alarmed brothers and sisters. There was no mother in the family. Mrs. Pollard had long vanished for a life of her own in another part of the country, and nobody was interested enough to go looking for her.

"He isn't there," Vallera said, when he returned to

Lew. He seemed oddly satisfied. "That means he's with Johnny, wherever the two of them are. Let's try the Gann girl."

"Flopsy?"

"Johnny's moll."

Lew wondered what he could do if they caught up with Johnny Broom. There was an implacable ferocity in Vallera that would be hard to stop. He knew what Vallera would try to do, and he was tempted to turn the car around and return to Precinct. If he did that, however, he'd have to tell the whole story, including the Comber business, and describing Vallera's present state of mind. He couldn't do that to Rose. He could only hope that the demons driving Tom on his night hunt wouldn't meet up with their victim.

Lew drove slowly, sending the prowl car drifting and ghosting down the sleeping streets. Usually, Lew liked these hours in the neighborhood. He kept the radio turned low, and every dispatch seemed to mention the widening search for Johnny Broom. The morning newspapers would have a field day, Lew thought. The murder of Henry Dexter Stephens, Chairman of the Governor's board on juvenile delinquency, the man labeled the city's best friend of youth—and now, murdered during an attempt to keep a youngster from crime—all this would make a story to rock the nation's press wires.

He and Vallera were right in the middle of it.

He listened to the muttering of the radio. Vallera acted like a killer himself, like a man with a single mania. Lew hoped and prayed their number would be called by the dispatcher to send them downtown before they came across Johnny.

He turned the corner and the patrol car drifted toward Flopsy Gann's house.

Vallera was the first to spot the boys coming out

of the alleyway just beyond.

His voice whispered with satisfaction.

"There they are."

His gun was in his hand before Lew could move.

Chapter Eleven

The sight of Vallera tumbling out of the patrol car only fifty feet away paralyzed Johnny Broom for an instant. Flopsy gave a small scream of terror. Stitch stumbled and tried to squeeze back into the alley, squawking with surprise, but Mike shoved him viciously, shouting: "Run, stupid! Run!"

His shove sent Stitch far out into the forefront, on the sidewalk. Vallera was already out of the car, hitting the pavement with his gun in hand, shouting something. Lew McGee yelled something, too, but Johnny couldn't make it out. Being taken by surprise like this was too shocking, too disastrous, to let him think. The sudden smashing report of Vallera's gun woke him from his paralysis.

"The graveyard!" he yelled.

He pushed Flopsy, and the girl ran ahead of him. Mike was close behind her. Vallera fired again, and Lew yelled once more. Lew had his gun out, but he didn't use it. Stitch fell to the pavement and Johnny tripped over him and they both went sprawling.

There was a note of amazement in Stitch's thin voice. "J-Johnny—I'm hit!"

Johnny hauled him to his feet.

"Run!" he said savagely.

Stitch ran, somehow. For all of his fat body, he was always the fastest runner in the gang. He kept up with Johnny as they skidded around the corner. A third shot woke clamorous echoes in the sleeping neighborhood. Lights were coming on in windows here and there, and he heard Vallera yell to them to halt, and he heard another shot, and then Johnny forgot everything in a panic burst of speed that put him beyond Stitch.

Mike and Flopsy were already around the next corner. Vallera was too ponderous to catch up with the fleet youngsters. And Lew McGee had turned back to the car to use the radio to spread the alarm. The auto graveyard where they always hid Stitch's wheels was two blocks north, another east. Johnny turned his head and saw Stitch stumble and fall; he whirled, grabbed him up again. His hands came away from Stitch's body wet and slippery with warm blood. The shock of it went through him like a hot knife.

"Stitch, man, keep going!" he pleaded.

"I—I can't ... my side hurts...."

"Try, man!"

Vallera's shout sounded dim behind them. Johnny dragged Stitch into a dark driveway, looked desperately around for a way to escape. A flight of stone steps, not more than six or seven of them, led to a series of backyards, with a narrow passage between them. He pulled Stitch that way, then crouched in the shadows.

"I—I feel sick, Johnny...."

"Shut up!"

Vallera went pounding past the driveway entrance. His squat, heavy body was like a dark nemesis, pursuing them. Johnny's throat felt as dry as a desert. His heart pounded crazily. He forced air in and out of his straining, swollen lungs.

The patrol car drifted by, and from their hiding place, Johnny saw Lew McGee lean from the window and call to Vallera. The spotlight on the patrol car slashed past their niche and moved on. Johnny lurched to his feet and pulled Stitch with him.

"Come *on!*"

"Let me—stay here," Stitch whispered.

"But they'll get you," Johnny argued fiercely. "Vallera will gun you down. You saw him, didn't you? You won't have a chance!"

"I don't care. I'm bleeding, Johnny...."

"I won't leave you, Stitch."

"Listen, I won't peel off any dope to the blues—if you're worried about that—"

Johnny said grimly: "I'm not worried. Because you're coming with me."

He forced Stitch to his feet. Stitch groaned and wavered. His usually strange, sweaty smell was worse, all at once. He held his side and staggered against Johnny, and Johnny helped him along. It was only a block to one corner of the auto junkyard. There was no sign of Mike or Flopsy. The patrol car had turned the corner and was out of sight.

The distance to the slot in the fence was a nightmare for Johnny. He didn't think he could make it, half-carrying Stitch. They had to hide again when the patrol car crossed the intersection ahead, cutting back and forth through the area. In a matter of minutes, Johnny knew, the place would be crawling with cops. He was tempted to drop Stitch, but he was afraid to. He had to keep Stitch with him. He wasn't sure why, but he had to.

It took several minutes before they were safely inside the area of rubble and rusting auto bodies. Johnny was forced to pause while Stitch rested. The bleeding went on, and the amount of it was frightening.

"Johnny, man—"

Johnny ignored him and called softly for Mike. Like a shadow of the night, Mike appeared, slim and dark, moving silently.

"How is he?" Mike asked.

"He's been shot in the side."

Mike looked coldly objective. "Maybe we ought to drop him."

"No," Johnny said. "We don't turn him over to the cops."

"Johnny, I hurt bad," Stitch whispered. "I need a doctor."

"Don't worry, we'll stop the bleeding." Johnny looked up as Flopsy came around the car. Her shadow was long and angular. She looked scared, and Johnny spoke harshly to her. "You got something you can use for bandages?"

"I ain't a nurse," Flopsy said.

"You're a nurse now. So fix him up."

"But we can't stay here!" Flopsy whined.

"Shut up and do what you're told."

Sirens wailed somewhere, the sound ululating up and up in a tight, alarming spiral. Flopsy tore a strip of white rayon from her underclothes and bent over Stitch. Johnny watched critically for a moment, then felt Mike pluck at his shirt. "You've got to have a plan, Johnny. You been thinking about what I suggested?"

"I don't know," Johnny said. "Your idea is crazy."

"You've got to do it more than ever now, if you insist on dragging Stitch with us."

Johnny looked at him angrily. "What are you hanging around for? Why don't you just take off and go back where you came from?"

"I'm in this with you, Johnny, and I want to help you."

"You must be nuts," Johnny muttered.

"Look, there isn't much time," Mike said. "You

need a cool pad, and quick, just for a couple of hours. The cops will crawl all over the neighborhood in a few minutes. They'll think of this place soon and surround it and search it. We can't stay here forever. You've got to go somewhere where they'll never dream of looking for you."

"But Vallera's house—!"

Mike's laugh was sardonic. "Can you think of a better place? Nobody will look for us in a cop's house!"

"But Rose is there—"

"So what's a dame?" Mike insisted. "We can handle her. That makes it even better—maybe we can use her for a hostage. How'd you like that, Johnny? You'd have the jump on that bastard old man of hers. He wants to kill you on sight, you know what. So we go into his home and grab his daughter and take her with us. Nobody will dare touch us then. You could bargain for anything you want, if it works."

"*If*," Johnny said dubiously.

"Think how it'll be!" Mike was strangely excited. "Hiding in Vallera's own pad, holding Rose—we could have some fun with her, Johnny-O." He saw Johnny's face change and added quickly: "I don't mean hurt her, man. Just scare her. We'd have a chance to figure things out, in the house, and maybe help Stitch. We could get what we need—maybe even grab Vallera when he comes in!"

"I'd like that," Johnny said bitterly. "I'd like to get that old son of a bitch. If he wasn't always riding my can, none of this would've happened."

"That's right," Mike said. "It's all Vallera's fault."

Flopsy stood up. She looked sick. "There's a big hole in Stitch's side. I think I got the bleeding stopped, but we need some medicine, some water for him. And some clean bandages."

"You see?" Mike said. "We need to get into somebody's house. So why not Vallera's?"

"I don't feel so good," Flopsy said. "I'm goin' home."

"You stay with us," Mike said quickly. "We all stick together, understand?"

"Don't tell me what to do!" Flopsy flared.

Mike slapped her. There was quick strength behind the blow, and Flopsy fell down. She lay awkwardly on her side, staring up at Mike with big eyes in a white, startled face. Then she started to get sick, throwing up on the rubble where she lay.

"You keep your mouth shut," Mike told her. "From now on, you just do what you're told."

Somehow, he had taken command.

Chapter Twelve

Mike felt bubbles of excitement lift in him until he seemed to soar over the city and the night. No other night had ever been like this. On other nights when he had prowled the Jungle, to perpetrate whatever indecencies happened to be convenient and safe, there had never been any real danger. He knew now that those other times had always been too easy. The risk and the danger here with Johnny Broom seemed to expand and sharpen all his senses. He had never felt so alive. He never had realized that this was what he had lacked before. He felt ten feet tall, invincible, a god who had come to earth to indulge his divine whims on the poor, stupid people who chanced his way. Sometimes in his dreams he had felt like this; but never before in reality. This danger was what he had always sought before, knowing surely that he could beat the unseen forces that malignantly surrounded him.

He cared nothing for Johnny, Stitch or Flopsy. They were pawns, susceptible to his suggestions. They were part of the set, the backdrops on the stage he had created. And there was still plenty of time to enjoy what was left of the night. There were a few hours yet. Plenty of time before thinking about getting home, slipping in the back way, maybe seeing Jane briefly, in her room up in the servants' quarters. Maybe tonight he'd give her what she always slobbered for, he thought. He felt generous. It would make a fitting climax for this best of all nights for him.

Mike laughed softly to himself. The first thing, of course, was to push these jerks to move as fast as possible, before the cops put a cordon around this place and their movement would be blocked.

He led the way, but it was Johnny Broom who showed him the route. From the auto graveyard they went up one alley, paused while a patrol car shot by, siren screaming, and then climbed a ladder to the roof of a row of attached houses. Stitch hampered them and needed help. The fat, straw-haired crum was losing blood again, and his breathing sounded funny, Mike noted. But he helped Johnny push and pull Stitch up the ladder, and then they moved the entire length of the block toward 7th Street, crossing from one connected roof to the other.

Vallera's house, being detached, with its small backyard, forced them to descend again. Johnny knew the way. He had hauled the homemade ladder along with them, and he lowered it now to a shed roof above the alley.

Flopsy went down first and waited below, her face a dim blur in the darkness beneath them.

The side of Vallera's house that faced them from

the roof was blank, solid brick, fronting on the narrow areaway between the corner house and the beginning of the row houses. Johnny couldn't see any lights, since he couldn't see either the front or back windows from here.

"Johnny, leave me here," Stitch whispered. "I can't get down that ladder."

"You got to get down," Johnny said. "We're almost there."

"I don't care." Stitch's face was a pale moon, pitted with his freckles. His eyes looked like enormous blind discs under his perspiration-wet, straw hair. "My side hurts, Johnny-O. Everything seems so far away, like when you got a fever...."

Mike said calmly to Johnny; "You can kill him right here, then, man."

"What?" Stitch whispered. He turned his head this way and that, as if he really couldn't see anymore. "What did you say?"

"You're a drag, man," said Mike, still calmly and softly. "We can't leave you here for the cops, don't you see?"

Stitch licked his lips.

"Listen, don't—"

"Then get down that ladder, you stupid bastard!" Somehow, Stitch made it.

The rest was easy.

Mike and Johnny went in first, through the back kitchen door that Rose had forgotten to lock.

Rose was upstairs in the front bedroom when she heard the footsteps moving around down below. She wore the thin pink robe and had thrust her small feet into summer mules. Sleep had escaped her, and she was sitting at the bow turret window, sipping iced coffee, resigned to waiting now until four o'clock in the morning for Tom and Lew to come off their tour of duty.

A small radio hummed softly beside her. She had heard about Henry Dexter Stephens, and for several minutes she had listened to the disc jockey's news announcement in a state of shock. It explained why Tom and Lew hadn't dropped by for their regular cup of coffee, anyway. Yet she couldn't believe it. She knew Johnny Broom, and she did not believe he could be a killer. Yet the news announcement alleged that he was.

Thunder rumbled in the night sky, but there was an arid feeling about the stale, hot air that moved sluggishly through the bow window, and she knew it would not rain.

The first thing she heard was the creak of a floorboard in the hallway at the foot of the stairs.

Then she heard someone groan.

The groan was followed by a fierce whisper for silence.

She stood up, and quick fear blossomed in her for Tom, for Lew, for the two men she loved and could not reconcile. Something had happened to one of them. One of them was hurt. Lew? Tom? She moved swiftly, silently to the door, then paused.

It didn't make sense. She had been sitting at the window just in order to watch the street for their patrol car. She hadn't seen the car approach.

She went back to the window and looked.

The street was empty.

All at once, the quality of her alarm changed. Rose was not a timid girl; you couldn't live in the Jungle and be timid, afraid of shadows. If you were afraid of anything, the object of your fears was always tangible—being mugged, perhaps, or raped by some hopped-up fool, or accosted by drunks. She had learned long ago how to cope with that sort of danger, and she was not given to girlish alarms.

But this was different.

Something was happening downstairs that she did not understand. There were people down there that she did not know.

Quickly, she turned to the bedroom door and listened. There was more whispering, another stifled moan. And something was knocked over in the darkness with a crash. Rose knew what it was—the glass-painted bowl lamp on the piecrust table in the dining room. She heard the sound of furniture being moved—the dining room table? Above and below all this, she heard the quick, hard hammering of her pulse.

She told herself to be calm and think. She had to be careful. Whoever was in the house hadn't come in by the front door, and Tom or Lew wouldn't come in any other way. The kitchen entrance, then. And all at once she remembered stepping out for a moment into the backyard. And she couldn't remember locking the kitchen door.

She could almost smell the danger rising up the dark stair well toward her.

Her first impulse was to hide, lock the front bedroom door, stay there, perhaps scream out of the window. But the lock was flimsy. It could be broken down in moments. And until she learned the real quality of the danger below, she knew better than to risk wild, drug-inspired violence.

She did not immediately connect the intrusion downstairs with what she had heard on the radio.

Living in the Jungle, however, had taught Rose that the first element in a situation of danger was to look to your self-defense. She stood silently, aware of the heat, the sounds downstairs, thinking about the extra revolver in her father's room in the back on the second floor. She knew exactly where it was, in the upper drawer of the old walnut bureau behind the doorway. She knew how to use it too—Tom had seen to that, long ago, taking her down to the police target ranges for practice. She was not afraid of guns, knowing what they were for, and she was a pretty fair shot.

The gun first, then.

She opened the bedroom door silently. She wanted to hurry because whoever was moving so clumsily downstairs would soon come up to investigate the bedroom floor. There wasn't much time. She walked down the carpeted hall to the head of the stairs and put her hand on the painted wooden banister rail. She could see the strange, colored gloom that filtered through the tinted, leaded glass of the front vestibule door, cast by the corner street lamp. A shadow moved across the faint shaft of light, head thrust forward, hair tangled, shoulders hunched. She couldn't tell who it was. She didn't even want to know, as yet.

The gun, the gun, she thought.

She began to tremble all at once as she stood at the head of the stairs, and she could have wept at the way her body betrayed her. She had to hold on tight to the newel post for moment. Now the voices were clearer, a boy's thin voice, girl's thinner voice. Her heart pounded.

"Hey, you up there!"

Someone was at the foot of the dark stairwell, looking up at her.

Rose gasped, whirled, ran for the back bedroom door. Footsteps pounded up the stairs after her. A scream lifted in her throat, but she couldn't get it out. Her fear choked her. She grabbed for the doorknob, missed in her haste, fumbled for it again. The footsteps were light, swift and sure, coming up behind her. Then she snatched the door open. She tried to close it behind her, but the fist of a hand thrust it back so that the edge struck her in the face, sent her staggering away. She still tried. The walnut dresser was right there in front of her. She lunged for it, panting, seeing the dark, slim figure slide into the room close behind her. In her haste, she pulled the wrong way, and the drawer stuck. She tugged at it again, pulled too hard, and the drawer came all the way out and fell from her fingers to the floor.

She saw the gun. The figure of the man (or was it a boy?) just stood there, watching her while she grabbed for the gun on the floor. He was so sure of himself he let her get her hand on it before he struck her.

The blow was hard and sharp across her face. Her breath whistled in her throat as she staggered. But she lifted the gun. He laughed and hit her again. The gun fell from her hand. He ignored it. She saw his thin, boyishly good-looking face in the gloom. He was laughing at her. She didn't know who he was. She had never seen him before. There was something wrong with his eyes, she thought dimly, something queer in the way he laughed and looked at her as he picked up the gun she had failed to get.

"Take it easy, lady," he whispered. "Don't yell or scream."

It was too late for that. She had sense enough to know this. Dizziness touched her, and she shrank back, away from him until she was in a corner of Tom's room and could move no further. Her face and her jaw hurt where he had struck her with his fist. Her mouth was bleeding. She forced her voice to remain level.

"Who are you? What do you want?"

"Just a little peace and quiet, sweetheart."

"I don't know you. You're not from around here, are you? Who's downstairs with you? Who—"

He hit her again, gratuitously. "You talk too much, sister."

She felt herself sliding to the floor, unable to control the weakness in her legs. She couldn't breathe. He hit her again and again, and she tried to crawl away from the pain, but it followed her remorselessly. The floor suddenly shook under her as someone ran up the stairs.

Then the pain stopped.

She heard a young, angry voice: "Leave her alone!"

"Look at this rod, Johnny."

"Where did that come from?"

"She was trying to get it."

"So now you've got it. Don't keep hitting her."

"She's Vallera's daughter, right?"

"Don't touch her again."

The voice said meaningfully: "Johnny, I've got a gun now too."

There was a pause. Then: "Let's get her downstairs."

She knew who had stopped the violence. She recognized Johnny Broom's voice. She wondered dimly what he was doing here in her house. Why had he come here? Tom and Lew and the whole police force were looking for him. He had committed murder tonight, little Johnny Broom had, little Johnny who wasn't little anymore, who had grown into something she no longer recognized or understood.

She felt his hands lifting her up.

"Come on, Rose."

"Johnny? Johnny Broom?"

"Yeah."

"You've gone crazy," she whispered. Her throat hurt, and it was hard to talk. "You're in terrible trouble."

"And you're gonna help me out of it, Rose."

"I? Don't you know what will happen when Tom gets back? He'll be here soon——"

"We know. We're waiting for him. Let's go downstairs. We got something for you to do."

No, she decided, she didn't know Johnny Broom anymore. But at least he had saved her from the violence of the other boy, the one who was a stranger. She let Johnny lead her downstairs.

She saw Flopsy Gann in the dining room, recognizing her from having seen her on the street. Flopsy had pulled the draperies closed in the dining room, shut the swinging kitchen door, and when she entered, Flopsy closed the tall walnut doors from the living room as well. Then someone put on the light over the dining room table and she saw Stitch Pollard.

She was not ordinarily a squeamish girl, but Rose felt suddenly sick and nauseated by the sight of Stitch's wound.

"Is he—he's been shot!"

There was blood on the dining room table, blood dripping to the carpeted floor. Stitch's face was round and pale, waxen. She saw the crude bandage plugging the hole in the boy's side and knew it was not enough. Stitch's eyes were closed, those pale, blind-like eyes that had been so arrogant earlier this evening when he had bumped into her on the sidewalk. His breath was quick and shallow, and his skin was wet with perspiration.

"He's been shot," Johnny Broom said. His voice was not normal, either. Rose looked quickly at the slender blond boy. His face was the face of a stranger, drawn, haggard, desperate. "Your old man shot him," Johnny said. "He tried to plug me and got Stitch instead."

Rose pulled herself together with a great effort, forgetting the pain she had just endured. "He needs help. Call a doctor."

The dark-haired one who had beaten her just laughed.

Johnny shook his head. "No calls. No doctor. You do it."

"But I—"

"Do whatever you can for him, Rose."

"But he's dying, can't you see?" she cried. "What's come over you, Johnny? No matter what you've done tonight, you can't just let your friend suffer like this! It—it's inhuman."

"That's me," Johnny muttered. "Inhuman. You heard the radio, Rose?"

"Yes," she admitted.

"So you know what chances I got of being taken alive."

"Johnny, this is crazy, you can give yourself up—"

"Shut up," said the dark-haired boy. "Get to work on Stitch. All women can handle stuff like that. Flopsy, go boil some water for the lady!"

Rose had recovered some of her poise. Her attention had moved outward, away from herself, to the two boys on their feet, to Stitch, groaning on the dining room table, to Flopsy, standing sullenly near the kitchen door. She felt revolted, but she kept her face and voice calm as she looked at the one who had hit her.

"Who *are* you?" she demanded of Mike.

Mike grinned. "Just a passing spectator, lady."

"The way you talk, you must come from a good family. You're not a friend of Johnny's. I've never seen you in this neighborhood before."

"I've been around, though," Mike said softly. "Now will you shut up and do something for Stitch or not?"

"I'll help him," Rose said. "Of course I'll help him."

She started for the kitchen, and Johnny said, "No lights."

"But I'll need some sulfa—I have some in a first-aid kit—and water and bandages."

"You can find them. Just feel around for them."

"I'll help the lady," Mike said, grinning. "I could use a drink, too. You got some rum in the joint, haven't you? I know the old man is a boozer. I've seen him plenty of times."

"You know a lot for a stranger in the neighborhood," Rose said flatly.

"And you're too damn curious, sister. Maybe I ought to work on you some more. It could be fun, baby."

"Go on," Johnny said. "Help Stitch."

Rose moved quickly into the darkened kitchen.

She didn't know what to do. She knew she dared not underestimate this new Johnny Broom with the haunted, desperate eyes. She wanted to help him, but she knew he would reject the slightest offer she made. And as for his friend—Rose knew, too, that here she was up against some unpredictable thing, something beyond the normal range of her experience, remembering the sadistic lust and joy he had taken in hitting her.

She worked quickly, not thinking of what her hands were doing as she groped in the cupboard for the first-aid box and got out scissors, gauze and several plastic envelopes of sulfa powder. She didn't know if that would be the right thing, but there was nothing else she could think of. They wouldn't let her call a doctor, and she knew, with a deep, heavy hopelessness, that Stitch Pollard was going to die. And Tom had killed him. Tom had shot the boy, done this to the young body, mutilating and tearing and killing it. She wondered if it had been necessary— and knowing her father and his grim hatred of the trouble-making boys in the neighborhood, she knew there must have been some other way of coping with this rather than gunfire. Her reaction swung violently one way and then another. She told herself not to think about it. She could dimly see the luminous hands of the kitchen clock on the yellow wall. It was three-thirty. Soon now, in half an hour, give or take five or ten minutes, Lew and Tom would park in front of the house in the patrol car. Lew probably wouldn't come in. But sometimes he lingered for a moment, smoking a cigarette. Tom would come in—

And then what would happen?

She knew a deeper terror at the thought than before. What did the boys hope to gain by breaking in here of all places? What did they plan to do?

She was sure they had a plan, however wild and improbable it might seem to her, if she could only learn its details—

Mike had found Tom's bottle of Cuban rum and was drinking greedily, thirstily. He held the gun he had taken from her loosely in his left hand. She wondered if she could snatch it from him. But then she remembered the obsessive way he had beaten her upstairs. She was afraid of him. She didn't know what he might do if she made a wrong move. She decided to wait.

Stitch was groaning and rolling around on the dining room table when she returned. Mike came back with the bottle, and Flopsy asked for a drink, and he looked at her for a moment, then abruptly handed it to her with a laugh of contempt. His thin, handsome face was flushed, his eyes were too bright, looking at Rose in her thin wrapper, her curved body not very well hidden by the clinging cloth.

Oh, God, Rose thought, *he might do anything....*

She kept herself busy working on Stitch.

Chapter Thirteen

Johnny prowled restlessly through the house. He had never been in Vallera's house before, and it seemed strange to him, after the rough and careless housekeeping Pete maintained in their own home. Everything seemed too neat, too shining and clean. When he came back to the dining room, Rose was finished bandaging Stitch. Her face was pale, but her eyes regarded Johnny steadily.

"If he doesn't get to a doctor soon, he's going to die, Johnny. I thought Stitch was your friend. Are you just going to let this happen?"

"Maybe your old man should've thought of that before he used his gun on Stitch, huh?" Johnny countered angrily.

"Did you think about anything when you shot Mr. Stephens?"

"He got in my way."

"Yes. And he was only trying to help you, Johnny!"

"Crap," Johnny said. "I never asked for any help from him."

"But you need it," Rose insisted. "You need help now."

Mike came out of the kitchen with a long carving knife and idly began marring the top of the dining table near where Stitch lay. Stitch seemed to be asleep or unconscious. Rose looked quickly at the long, cruel gouges Mike was making in her fine polished furniture and she opened her mouth to speak in protest, met Mike's pale, mocking eyes, and thinned her mouth, and turned back to Johnny. "How long do you think you can keep this up? If you're afraid that my father won't give you a chance to surrender safely, let me call the police station and explain about it. You'll be safe, then."

"Yeah. For the chair," Mike said.

Rose didn't look at the second boy. She kept her eyes on Johnny, trying to persuade him by sheer mental force. Johnny looked at her and said: "I'm not giving myself up. And the only help you can give me is by shutting up."

"Maybe she has some money," Mike suggested.

"Do you?" Johnny asked.

She bit her lip. "A little. Upstairs."

"Let's get it," Johnny said.

He waved the gun at her and she led the way up to the second floor. Mike was starting to work with his knife on the drapes and wallpaper when they left. Upstairs, in the front room, Rose opened a dresser drawer and took out her purse. Johnny grabbed it with his left hand (he still held the gun in his right) and then he walked over to the bowed window to examine its contents by the light that came in from the street lamp.

Rose's voice was calm. "There are only eighteen dollars in there, Johnny."

He counted the bills and thrust the money in his pocket and threw the purse savagely to the floor. "That ain't enough."

"There's no more in the house. I'm sorry."

His head snapped up. "Sorry?"

"I'd like to help you, Johnny. Truly, I would."

"That's a fat lie," he scoffed. "You're like all the rest of them. Talk, talk, talk! Go on, get downstairs."

"Wait a moment, Johnny. I want to talk to you about your friend. Who is he, anyway?"

"Mike? He's nobody."

"You know that isn't so. He tries to talk the way you do, but he's been well-educated, as if he went to a private school. What is he doing here, with you?"

"I don't know," Johnny said.

"Was he with you when you—" She couldn't say it. "Was he with you all night?"

"Yeah."

"Don't you know his last name?"

"No."

"There's something wrong with him, Johnny. You can see that, can't you? Perhaps he's the one who got you into this."

Johnny laughed thinly, "No. I chopped Stephens with my own little hatchet. What are you worried about Mike for, anyway?"

"He frightens me," Rose said. "I'm not ashamed to admit it."

Johnny didn't reply. For the first time, peering through the bowed windows, he noticed a light on in his own house, shining in the window of Pete's bedroom upstairs. He swung back to Rose.

"Is my brother home?"

"Yes."

"Is he all right?"

"Some men took him home. They've gone now."

"You sure?"

"I saw them go," Rose said. It was a lie, and she wasn't sure why she thought it best to lie about that. Perhaps they were gone anyway. There were no cars parked on the street now. She drew a deep, uncertain breath. She felt less afraid, being alone with Johnny, no matter how unfamiliar he now was. "Johnny, what are you going to do with me?"

"I ain't decided yet."

"You know me, Johnny. We've been friends for a long time, haven't we?"

He turned his head to look at her. He was still thinking about Pete over there. Now he remembered his thoughts when he had seen her hours ago, before dark, on the street, comparing her mature body to Flopsy, sensing her cleanliness, the soft flesh under the thin wrapper she hugged around herself. His eyes darkened in the shadows of the bedroom.

"Haven't we, Johnny?" Rose insisted.

His answer came slowly, forced with pain from the truth he knew. "I have no friends anymore. Nobody in the world."

"That's not so. I—"

"Shut up. I'm trying to think."

She persisted. "How long do you think you can stay in this house? My father will be home soon—"

"That's what I'm waiting for," he said meaningfully.

She looked at the gun in his hand. "Johnny, you can't—"

"I want his car," Johnny said.

"A *police* car?"

"It will get me out of town," he said.

"Who's crazy idea is that? Mike's? You're smarter than that, Johnny. You'll never make it."

"Yes, I will. Because you and your old man will come with me, see? It's simple, sister. And if either of you try something funny, I'll kill you both. You first."

She looked at him and believed what he said. She had been wrong, she thought. She had almost been sure she still knew Johnny, this boy she had seen every day of his life, playing in the street, going to school, growing up. But she didn't know him. He had changed. He was a stranger. A boy with a gun.

Her fear expanded for Tom and Lew. There was no telling what Johnny planned, or what Mike would egg him on to doing. She had to get away, now, before it was too late, and something awful happened here. She turned her head sharply as something crashed downstairs. It was Mike, she decided, wandering along his path of vicious vandalism. She closed her eyes and tried to pretend that the destruction the boy was spreading down there didn't even mean anything to her. Perhaps it didn't. It was the senselessness behind the vandalism that had significance.

She closed her eyes, and at the same time she became aware of the low, murmuring throb of a car engine below the window. At the same moment, a low warning whistle came from the foot of the stairs below. She looked at Johnny Broom. He stood flat against the wall beside the window, peering down at the street through the thin summer curtains. There were no screens on the bow turret windows, and the sash was up. The sound of the car came with sharp familiarity into the darkened bedroom. It was Tom and Lew. They were a little early. But they were here. She didn't have to look to know that it was Tom's patrol car down there by the curb.

Johnny raised his right hand slowly, the gun pointing at the ceiling for a moment. His stare was intent on the street. Rose even heard the faint murmuring of the police radio in the car now. Her heart began to pound erratically, and she forced herself to draw a deep slow breath and then she moved toward Johnny. He didn't look at her. He seemed to have forgotten for the moment that she was with him. There was a strange, feral look on his face—a combination of murderous fear and anger.

A car door thudded. Rose stopped. Three more steps, and she would be at the window, too. She heard Lew's voice say something, but she couldn't make out the words. Johnny was a lean, flat shadow against the wall beside the window.

Rose thought of Mike hiding downstairs with the gun he had taken from her. She imagined, all in a moment, what was going to happen. Johnny was up here, and he couldn't stop Mike. Maybe he wouldn't want to anyway. But Tom would come in the front door, not suspecting, not dreaming of his danger. And the danger was there, like the peril from a wild animal, ravening through the city streets.

She couldn't let it happen.

And then, an instant before she could make herself jump for Johnny's gun, she heard a sudden renewed squawking from the radio in the car down there. Lew called something in an urgent voice to Tom on the sidewalk. Footsteps scraped on the pavement. The car door slammed again. Johnny began to curse in a flat, hopeless voice.

"They're not coming in!" He sounded incredulous. "They're going away again!"

Now, Rose thought.

She leaped for the gun in Johnny's hand, and at the same moment, she opened her mouth to scream a warning to Tom and Lew. The scream never came out. Johnny's move was just a blur in the shadows. Too late, she knew that he had been watching her as anxiously as he had watched the men on the street below. She was aware of smashing, unbelievable pain across her face as he hit her with the gun. She felt fingers claw at her throat, throttling the scream she had tried to get out. His swift fury was incredible. She felt him hit her again, but this time it seemed as though the flesh that cried in pain was not here, but belonged out somewhere in the darkness that swirled around her. She knew she had fallen to the floor. She felt him kick her, and tried to cry out again, and then his weight came down on her, his body falling on her. Something thumped on the floor. His gun? She tried to find it, but she couldn't move. She was pinned down by the weight of his hard, sweaty body.

Tears sprang to her eyes, and she squeezed them away, felt them slide down her cheeks. Her nose was bleeding. She could taste the warm saltiness of her blood in her mouth. And then, incredibly, she felt the hungry, hard, inexpert passion of his kiss.

Moaning, she threw her head to one side, trying to escape him. She heard his soft laughter.

"I always went for you, baby," he whispered.

"Johnny—"

"I got nothing to lose," he gasped.

She tried to roll away from under him. He slapped her face once, twice, three times.

"Think you're too good for me?" he panted. "I'll show you, you bitch, you copper's bitch—"

"Please—"

He was too strong for her. Her body went limp, spent under his hard, lithe weight. Dimly, she heard footsteps running up the stairs toward them. But it didn't matter. Nothing mattered anymore. Lew, she thought, her mind crying, weeping the words, *we waited too long....*

Her lack of struggle took Johnny by surprise. He sprawled across her, uncertain, wary of a trick. She felt him reach out beyond her on the floor somewhere and recover the gun he had dropped. It didn't matter. The patrol car had gone away. Tom and Lew were safe for the moment. But they would come back. And the next time they would walk in, unprepared, to face the two boys....

"Hey, man...."

It was Mike's voice. Rose felt Johnny rise quickly, releasing her. Mike said something she didn't understand, and Johnny answered in a rapid, angry tone. Mike argued about it. There was a dull, pulsing roar in Rose's ears that covered the meaning of their words, but she felt certain they were arguing over her. She didn't care. She was aware only of the pain in her face, of the blood on her mouth and cheek, where Johnny had hit her. But neither pain nor blood anywhere else. Then she became aware of her semi-nakedness and rolled away, toward the bed, expecting hard hands to seize her momentarily.

But nobody touched her.

And then she understood what Mike was telling Johnny.

Stitch Pollard was dead.

Chapter Fourteen

"You take it easy," Johnny said to Rose.

It was a few minutes later. He stood watching her as she bathed her face in cold water in the bathroom, and he wondered why he hadn't gone through with the sudden, lustful instinct that had taken hold of him. She had put on a cotton dress, and her eyes looked queer and strange when they met his stare in the mirror, wary of him, as he lounged in the bathroom doorway.

"Stitch might have lived, if you'd gotten a doctor for him," she said finally.

He shrugged. "So we didn't. So he's dead. He was a smelly crum, anyway."

"He was your friend. He idolized you, Johnny."

"He was a jerk."

"Yes," Rose said meaningfully. "Yes, I suppose he was."

It didn't touch him. He was beyond her words now. He had gone somewhere beyond all human and decent contact. Johnny knew this as well as Rose, but it didn't bother him. It made him feel better, he decided, because it made what had to be done next all the easier. He knew that this was the only way he could live from now on—alone, acknowledging no rules, no other man's laws, no restraints except those he chanced to place on himself. That was the way it had to be, because he wasn't going to go soft now and give himself up. Not with Comber, the Lancers, the cops, and everybody in the city hunting for him, ready to gun him down. It was easier, knowing there was nobody left who mattered except himself.

It was almost four o'clock in the morning. Soon church bells would start to ring and people would begin to move around again in the daylight. He still needed money, he still needed a car. There was no telling now if old man Vallera and Lew would come back. Time was running out, and he felt its pressure like a hand squeezing at the back of his neck. Even now, there was no relief from the heat. The thunder still rolled tantalizingly around the edge of the horizon, reminding him of the crash of bowling balls at Sandor's Alleys. It seemed a long time ago, when he had gone there with the Lancers, in another time and another world. A place he could never find again.

Johnny turned away abruptly and went back to the front room. He knew he didn't have to worry about Rose raising an alarm again. She had learned her lesson. She knew what would happen if she tried anything. It was marked on her face, a thing in her eyes that hadn't been there before.

He listened to the sound of Flopsy weeping somewhere, and he was touched by irritation. What in hell was she bawling about? Stitch never meant anything to her. It had been a mistake to drag Flopsy along in this, the way she got shook up. But there hadn't been any choice. Flopsy knew too much. And she'd be useful for a little while longer anyway. Then he'd get rid of her. He hadn't decided just how. Maybe he'd just dump her out on a lonely road somewhere. She wasn't important.

He saw that Pete had turned out the lights in the bedroom of his house across the street. Maybe Pete could help. There was money in the house, money Pete tucked away like a goddam stupid squirrel, loose cash here and there. Fifty, sixty, maybe a hundred bucks. Every little bit would help.

The more he thought about it, the more fruitful the idea seemed. It would only take five, ten minutes to get in there, once he got across the street and up on the roofs. The way was as familiar to him as the palm of his hand. There wouldn't be any danger. He knew every pitfall, and he would be careful.

He went downstairs and told Mike about it. He was shocked by what Mike had done to the inside of the house, and then amused. Mike had abandoned the knife and found some cans of paint in the kitchen. Bright yellow and green daubs made a crazy pattern on the furniture and walls of the front living room. The place was a real gone mess. Mike idly splashed initials on a piecrust table while Johnny explained what he was going to do. *M.S.T.* Johnny wondered what the "T" stood for, but his curiosity did not linger.

Mike looked at him with flat eyes. "Think you can make it?"

"Sure," Johnny said. "The whole thing will take

only a few minutes. There's a hundred bucks, easy, in my house. Pete will give it to me."

"You hope."

"Don't worry about Pete and me," Johnny said. "You just keep things under control here."

Mike grinned wolfishly. "You trust me with that Rose? She's a real likely piece, man. A little old, but stacked, man."

"Leave her alone for now," Johnny said. "Keep your eye out for old Vallera."

Mike nodded. There was something in the way he looked that made Johnny hesitate, but then he decided he didn't give a damn what Mike did here, so long as he stayed alert. He went out through the back kitchen door, not looking at Stitch lying so quietly on the dining room table.

It took less than ten minutes for Johnny to cross the street, climb the shed roof behind Feeney's Candy Store, and from there use the wooden ladder to the tar and gravel roofs of the row houses, stepping lightly from one to another in the darkness. He paused for a long time at the hatchway to his own house. The sky was like a huge black bowl, pressing down around his head. From up here, he could see the sheets of heat lightning flickering and flashing on the western horizon, making a weird silhouette out of the rooftops and chimneys he could see.

He opened the hatch carefully and listened for several more minutes. The thing he had feared, the sound of a cop's voice maybe talking to Pete, or the slight shift or groan of old wooden flooring that would mean a cop waiting in the dark, a trap for him—none of this could he sense. The house was empty except for Pete. They hadn't expected Johnny Broom to come home.

He lowered his legs into the hatch opening, hung

there for a moment, and then dropped lightly into the darkness, to the upper hallway floor. His feet made quick, twin thudding sounds as he fell into a crouch. The gun was in his hand. The darkness was absolute. He held his breath and listened. There was no alarm.

After a moment he could see that the door to Pete's front bedroom was open. No air stirred through the house. There was the smell of Pete's cooking, of perspiration-soaked clothes, of familiar wood and dust and furnishings. The smell of the only home he had ever known. He pushed it out of his mind and advanced toward Pete's room.

"Johnny?"

The whispered voice hit him like a club. The breath jumped and whistled in his throat as he whirled. The gun was up. He saw Pete standing in the bathroom door.

"I heard you on the roof, Johnny," Pete said.

"Oh."

"What did you came back here for?"

"Are you alone?"

"Just me and my shadow," Pete said. He added quickly, "That's a joke, Johnny-O. We're alone in the house, all right. I had a feeling you'd come back this way. I was listening for you." Pete's voice was neither friendly nor unfriendly. It was a nothing. It sounded flat, as if he had to make an effort to speak around swollen lips and broken teeth. He said again: "What did you come back for?"

"Maybe just to say good-bye," Johnny whispered.

"Good-bye, then."

Johnny stared at Pete's big figure. The dumb ox, why was he standing there like that? He ought to be in bed. Johnny could see the bandages on his head, coming down under his chin, and the way the bandages shone white across the black, springy hairs on Pete's broad chest.

"Just like that?" he said.

"Good-bye and good luck."

Johnny drew a shaken breath. "I need some money, Petey-O."

"No."

"You got some. I need it. I'm your brother, you got to help me!"

The flat unnatural voice slapped at him. "After what you did to Mr. Stephens?"

"I couldn't help it. How much money have you got, Petey?"

"And after what you tried to pull on me? You call me your brother, right? And you and that punk, crazy kid you were with were ready to kill me. So now you come crawling back here for help. You must be out of your mind."

"No lectures, man. Just the money, huh?" Johnny said tightly. The way Pete just stood there was getting on his nerves. He began to be sorry he had come here after all. "I know you got eighty, a hundred bucks hidden around this dump. Shake it up, huh?"

"I've got six dollars," Pete said. "If you want it, you'll have to take it off me."

He walked past Johnny and went down the hallway, limping oddly, and went into his bedroom. He started to close the door in the darkness, and all at once Johnny leaped after him, rage burning in his head like a red flame, and slapped the door open with a stiff hand. Pete was sitting down on the edge of the bed. The light was better here, sliding in from the street. Pete looked like an old, old man—what little Johnny could see of his bandaged face. His eyes were just dark pits, like dead coals, under his bushy black brows.

Pete's sigh moved like a ghost in the hot, roughly

furnished room.

"I don't know what to do about you, Johnny."

"You told the cops it was me, didn't you?" Johnny snapped.

"No. But they know, anyway."

"They know because you told them."

"Maybe I should have," Pete said. "I don't know. I've tried everything I could with you. I'm not smart. You're smarter than me, you always were. Too smart for your own good, and now you're going to die of it."

"They won't get me," Johnny said flatly.

"You'll never make it, kid."

"I'll make it if you cough up the money."

Pete said, "I'll swap you the money for your gun. That's the best deal I can think of. Give me the gun and you can have the money. And I'll give you a half hour before I call the cops on you."

Johnny stared down at his brother's big, broken body. He didn't believe this was Pete talking. He didn't understand it. Pete was dumb, all right, but he was playing this cool, this time, he didn't seem to know that Johnny was ready to do anything to get the money. It was just like always, Johnny thought, rage slowly kindling in him again. You could never get through to Pete and make sense to him. He was like an elephant, a dumb ox, too stupid to move when you goaded him, too obstinate to get out of your way.

He suddenly stepped forward and pushed at Pete's shoulder to make him look up. "Six bucks, you said. For the gun? You're lying about the money. You got more, haven't you?"

"For my insurance, yeah."

"Where is it? And how much?"

"Like you said. Eighty-seven dollars."

"Where?"

Pete said flatly, "I won't give it to you, Johnny."

Johnny said, speaking with care, "Pete, you listen to me. I'm in trouble, and I'm not going to let the cops take me. No matter what, you understand? I need money. I can get a car. I'm going away and you'll never hear from me again. That what you want? You give me the money and I'll just go away, and that'll be that. Right? You got that, stupid? You understand? No fuss or feathers, just give it to me."

"And if I don't?"

"I'll take it."

"Go ahead, use the gun on me," Pete said.

Johnny felt a sudden flash of anger that was beyond his control. His hand shot out, and the sound of his slap against Pete's face was loud, like a gunshot. Pete fell back, and a dark stain promptly began to spread under the white of his bandages. His eyes were dark and blank, looking up at Johnny from the bed.

"Try it again," he whispered. "You're no brother of mine. You might as well kill me."

Johnny's breath came in great, pumping gasps as he tried to control his anger and his hatred. Sweat dripped from his face. It was very quiet in the room, except for the sound of their breathing. The gun felt slippery in his hand. He wanted to kill Pete. Put the dumb ox out of his misery. Beat him to a pulp. But he knew that wouldn't do any good. The way Pete was now, he could beat him up good and get away with it. For the first time. And the last. But that was small satisfaction now. He knew that Pete's stubbornness and dullness was something he couldn't move. Like knocking your head against a brick wall. He couldn't get through to him.

He thought desperately of running through the house, tearing it apart, hunting for the money. But time was running out. He felt as if he were falling down those dark steps faster and faster, with no way to stop himself. He wanted to yell, he wanted to sit down and cry. He did neither. He controlled himself with one great tremendous effort.

"All right, Pete. Keep your money. I'm going."

"Good-bye," Pete said again.

"You going to call the blues on me?"

"No."

"How come? You help me with that, but not with dough! How come? You don't make sense."

"I'll think of you as my brother," Pete said heavily, "until the sun comes up."

"You're shook," Johnny said. "I don't get it."

"You never will," Pete said. "Because part of it is my fault. Mr. Stephens' blood is on my hands, too. I promised I'd take care of you, and I tried. Sure, I'm dumb. I didn't know how to do it. But I should have seen where you were going, and if I could've seen it, maybe I could have stopped it. Now it's too late. And part of the fault is mine. I don't know how it happened, kid. I tried my best. But it wasn't good enough. You and me look at things from different angles. You don't live in the same world with me. You've got no roots, no home, no loyalties. I tried to give you a home, but it wasn't enough. So go on, now. I won't call the cops. But I won't help you with money, either."

Johnny licked his lips. Pete's voice was somehow frightening. He tried one last maneuver. "You don't give me the money, I'll get it someplace else. Maybe I'll have to kill somebody else for it."

Pete looked at him and said nothing.

"So it will be your fault if I kill another guy, Pete. Is that the way you want it?"

"I've said my last word," Pete told him.

Johnny waited in the bedroom doorway. He thought Pete might change his mind. But Pete lay down on the rumpled, twisted sheets on the bed and folded his hands under his battered head and looked up at the ceiling and didn't say any more. He didn't even pay any attention to the blood that dripped through the bandage from the wound that Johnny's blow had reopened.

Chapter Fifteen

Mike began to get jittery. With Johnny gone, he began to feel different about being here in the cop's house. He forced Rose and Flopsy to sit side by side on the couch in the old front "parlor" while he watched from the window, surveying the dark and empty street. Johnny was taking a long time about getting the money from his brother. Maybe he'd walked into trouble over there; maybe the cops had been sent for. It would be ridiculous, Mike thought, if he were caught here like this, and when he thought of that possibility, his nerves tightened even further. Whatever happened, he had to think of himself, plan his way out, the route home to the safety of Society Hill.

He walked over to where Rose sat on the couch. Even with her bruised face and puffy mouth, where Johnny had hit her, she was quite a piece. He thought of Jane, and all the other women who had called him "cute" and had touched him and had gone on from there with him. There had never been one like Rose. The sight of her began to excite him.

"Hey," he said. "When does your old man come home?"

Rose answered flatly. "He's overdue now."

"You figure he's going to handle things, huh? You think he can take us?"

"I don't know," she said truthfully.

He made a sweeping gesture with the gun in his hand, exhibiting the vandalism in the room, and laughed. "How do you like my new decorations? Fancy, huh? Your furniture was pretty cheesy, you know?"

"My father always said boys like you were like animals," Rose said quietly. "I used to argue with him about it. I used to say that society was at fault, that there was too much confusion, or lack of discipline, and boys like you simply reflected that confusion."

"Yeah?" Mike was interested. "So what do you think now?"

Rose lifted her head and looked at him. "You could be a nice boy," she said. "I can guess at your background."

"Yeah?" Mike moved in quick, spastic gestures. Where was Johnny? Why didn't he come back? He said, "So tell me more."

"But no such excuses like confusion or poor discipline or lack of opportunity can apply to a boy like you."

"What are you, a social worker, or something?"

"I'm just trying to understand you," Rose said. "Is it just excitement? Do you hate people? If you do, why?"

Mike laughed. "I like excitement. It makes me feel big."

"Bigger than everybody?"

"That's right."

"But it's only the gun that makes you feel that way. How would you feel without the gun? Or if you weren't as strong as you are?"

He saw at once what she was leading up to. "You think it's just the gun, huh? Is that it?"

"Most of it," Rose said.

He laughed inwardly. "And if I put the gun down, you think you could handle me, sister? You think I'd have to let you go?"

"I'd have an even chance. That would make the danger greater to you. But you only like danger you're sure you can handle. You're not big or brave. You're not even a man. Without the gun, you're just a scared, lost boy."

"A kid who's all shook up, huh?"

"Yes."

He walked across the room and threw the gun down the hall, toward the dining room. He knew she heard it hit the inner door down there. He saw the way her face changed, the way the tip of her tongue crept out speculatively, to moisten her swollen lip. Her eyes touched the front door, then swung quickly away. He knew she was measuring the distance she would have to jump.

"I'm still big," he said. "With or without the gun."

She went for it. As long as she had kept sitting there passively on the couch, he hadn't been able to figure out how to begin with her. He wanted to do what Johnny had almost done, fighting for it, only he wouldn't leave off until he was finished with her. She thought she was so smart! Needling about the gun, about not being a man unless he had the rod.

When she moved in her desperate gambit for freedom, lunging up from the couch for the front door, he was instantly in action, crashing into her.

Vallera finished the small, half-pint bottle of rum he had secreted under the seat of the patrol car. There was nothing about him to show that the liquor had had any effect. Lew hung up the radio phone as Vallera popped a mint into his mouth and began grinding it up slowly between his strong jaws.

"False alarm," Lew said. "The pickups weren't our boys. Broom is still loose."

"They're not just boys now," Vallera snapped. "They're killers."

Lew said bluntly, "Are you through with that bottle?"

"Yeah."

"How long do you think I can cover you, Tom?"

"Nobody asked you to cover me."

"What is it with you, anyway?" Lew said. He turned the patrol car back toward 7th Street, not even thinking about it. So far, no call had come through for them to report down to the Hall. Evidently the powers-that-be hadn't been able to locate the District Attorney as yet. And their trick would soon be over. Johnson and Al Bowen would take over the car, after he dropped off Vallera and returned to Precinct. Maybe they would have to put in overtime, anyway, the way things were, though. Lew felt tired now, weary to his bones with the heat, the long night, the exhausting hunt for Johnny Broom. And he was tired of Vallera, of the man's stubborn and dangerous ferocity, his contempt and cruelty, and his drinking. He said again, "You've only got a year to go for pension time, Tom. Tonight, of all nights, you must be crazy to hit the bottle like this."

Vallera looked carved of stone, monolithic, on the seat beside him. His whisper was harsh. "I know that. But I can't help it."

"You know it's been getting worse lately," Lew said.

"I know, I know."

"Does Rose realize how bad it is?"

Lew didn't know if Vallera would bother to reply, and he was surprised by the heavy patience in the older man's voice. "Rose has got a pretty good idea. But don't give me any lectures, McGee. From you, a rookie still wet behind the ears, I don't think I could stand it."

"There's got to be a reason for it," Lew insisted. "What's eating you, anyway?"

Vallera turned his head and looked at him. "Why should you worry about me? You hate my guts, right?"

"No," Lew said. "Not really. You give me a rough time, but I admire lots of things about you. You're a good cop." It cost him a tremendous effort to say this and admit it, knowing it was true; and he was glad that for some reason he was able to say it at last. "I've learned a lot from you, Tom."

Vallera made a noise in his throat. He sounded suddenly thoughtful. "I never gave you much of a chance, I guess. Are you really in love with Rose?"

"Yes. You know I am."

"You know I don't want to lose her. You understand about that?"

"She has her own life to live," Lew insisted. "She has a right to be free. You can't keep her tied to you forever; and in any case, I don't see why you insist on thinking you'll lose her when we get married. You wouldn't, you know."

Vallera sighed and cursed softly. "I got too many things on my mind lately. I guess you know what. It's not just Rose, either. It's everything. The whole goddam, crazy, mixed-up world. I fell off the merry-go-round somewhere, and I've never been able to climb back on again. It's been since the war, I guess, when things started to change, and I couldn't change with it. Young fellows like you, veterans, going to college in your spare time, wearing the uniform. And punks like Johnny Broom to handle. They just don't make sense to me. I can't figure what's gotten into everybody. In the old days, black was black and white was white. You knew the law, and it was either broken or not. You never had to be afraid of slapping down a punk when he got out of line. You didn't have ten thousand do-gooders screaming about a kid's psychowatchamacallit in court. If he committed a crime in the old days, he got sentenced to prison or reformatory for whatever penalty the law provided. But it's different today. A cop is more likely to be called on the carpet for manhandling some brat who tried to stick a knife in him. And a man don't know where he stands anymore."

"So you drink and hope that'll make it all go away?" Lew asked gently.

"Something like that, I suppose," Vallera said. "I don't know how to figure things anymore. Like tonight, I've got to get this Johnny Broom. You know he was at that warehouse; you know he gunned down Henry Stephens. The best friend those kids ever had— a Johnny Broom kills him. And he got away from me twice. How is that going to look down at the Hall? Is a punk like that smarter and sharper than me? I know the neighborhood, I know these young hoods. I ought to be able to outsmart him easily. But I lost him. I know he's around here somewhere, still nearby, but now I just don't know where to look."

Lew stopped the car in front of Vallera's house. The street was dark and empty. Vallera got out with a heavy, tired motion, and for several moments he stood in squat, solid pensiveness, as though rooted to the sidewalk, staring at his house.

"You think they'll call us down to the Hall before

the tour is over?" Lew asked.

"Probably first thing tomorrow. And they'll lift my potsy."

"Maybe not," Lew said.

"You never been on the carpet down there, so you don't know how it can be. A man like Stephens gets killed under you, and they don't let you open your mouth to talk. They *tell* you how wrong you are and what mistakes you made. Either you bring in the killer, or it's the ash can for you."

"Want me to go inside with you?" Lew asked.

"I won't be a minute. I got a feeling—those punks in the neighborhood, and all, with rods—I just want to make sure Rose is asleep all right," Vallera said.

"I'll wait here, then," Lew said.

Sergeant Tom Vallera went slowly up the steps, fumbled with his key, opened the door, and walked into the dark house.

Johnny Broom didn't see the red patrol car until he dropped like a cat to the shed roof behind Feeney's candy store. He was no more than thirty feet at that moment from where Lew McGee sat waiting behind the wheel. He remained as he was, in a crouch, hidden in the shadows of the board fence. Lew was looking the other way, toward Vallera's front door, his head cocked a little to one side to catch the murmured signals on the police radio.

Johnny felt the butt of Comber's gun jabbing up under his ribs from its snug position in his belt. He took it out. His heart slowed and stopped its crazy hammering when he felt the gun's weight and solidity in his hand. It was a tough break, being away from the house just when the blues returned. But maybe Mike could handle the old man, Vallera. Maybe it would work out all right, anyway.

He held the gun up and straightened, measured the distance across the street to the patrol car, and then in a smooth burst of speed, he raced silently across the pavement toward the driver's side, where Lew still sat with his head turned the other way.

Mike was ready. He'd heard the car stop, and he jumped up, leaving Rose as she was on the floor. Flopsy was asleep on the couch and hadn't moved at all for the last five minutes. The pod had finally reached her and taken her off to some private never-never land of her own. Anyway, Flopsy didn't count, Mike thought. He looked down at Rose and saw the silver traces of tears on her battered face, where the light from the street came through the bow windows and touched the floor. He didn't know if she had passed out cold or not.

If Rose heard the car stop, she gave no sign of it. She didn't move. Mike turned away and flattened in the shadows beside the inner vestibule doors, just on the other side of the big, old-fashioned, ceramic umbrella stand.

He heard the cop shuffle up the outside steps and pause and hunt for his keys. He held the gun ready. He wasn't afraid. He felt cold, cold clear through, a thing of ice. He didn't even breathe.

He hadn't quite figured it would work out like this. He would rather have had Johnny do this sort of thing, so he could watch and enjoy it, without really being a part of it. But there was no help for it now. It was too late to turn and run. The danger in that was too great.

Vallera's shadow was thick and black on the floor just inside the entry, where the street light seeped in around his figure. He closed the door and most of the light was cut off. Then he came through the double inner doorway and saw Rose first thing, a dim shape, on the floor of the living room.

He made a small sound in his throat, the beginning of a cry of anguish, and Mike emerged from his niche behind the door at his back and struck hard.

The butt of Mike's gun smashed through the uniform cap on Vallera's head.

The cop went down to his knees. He made a strangled, coughing sound. A look of surprise and fury congested his face. His cap fell off and rolled across the rug toward his daughter.

Mike hit him again.

And again.

A desperate fury possessed him, compounded with fear. The cop wouldn't lay still. He kept trying to crawl away and scrabbled for the gun in his holster. His mouth was a dark hole that made cursing and moaning noises. His eyes were the worst part of it, glaring up at Mike's slim, dark figure with a hatred that seemed able to kill. Mike dropped to his knees, panting and sweating. He reversed the gun, got his finger on the trigger, smashed the muzzle up under the old guy's chin. Even then, the bastard wouldn't stop trying to get away. Mike didn't understand it. The old man wasn't afraid of him. All it would take was a little squeeze on the trigger.

But he knew the sound of it would break up everything.

He reversed the gun again and beat twice more at the straining, inhuman head that kept struggling to rise up from the floor.

Chapter Sixteen

The first hint of danger that came to Lew was the cold jab of the gun muzzle behind his ear. He didn't move. His hands were on the car wheel, and he kept them that way, in plain sight. The shock of being taken by surprise like this was what saved him. Later, he knew that the slightest gesture at that moment would have been his last.

"Johnny?" he whispered.

"That's right. You're smart, Lew. Stay just like that."

"All right. What do you want?"

"Get out of the car," said Johnny. "Quick."

Lew got out and stood in the middle of the street. The street was empty and asleep. There was nobody to see what was happening. Even if somebody saw it, there would be no help. Not from the people living around here. He kept his hands up, shoulder high. In his mind, a dozen alternative courses of action stumbled over each other, remembered from the judo classes at police school, the tactics to be followed in situations like this. All very well, Lew thought; but Johnny Broom was too smart. Reflex action could trigger the gun in Johnny's hand, anyway. And Lew knew, with a cold fear, that he was very close to death.

"Take it easy, Johnny, you hear?" Lew said. "Don't do anything foolish." He heard the sound of his voice as if somebody else had spoken the words—somebody quietly detached from the ugly, clamoring panic he felt.

Johnny reached around him and flipped the police revolver from Lew's holster and tossed it to the front seat.

"Get the keys now," Johnny said.

Lew reached in and took the keys from the ignition lock. He could have made a try for the gun then, but he didn't dare. He held the keys in his hand and straightened up again. "I don't understand this, Johnny," he said. "You should have been miles from here by now."

"That just what you cops would figure. So I'm not," Johnny said. "Let's go inside."

"In Vallera's house?" Lew felt confused. There was something more to it, then. His first thought was that all Johnny wanted was the patrol car to help make his getaway. The keys made sense out of that idea. But evidently that wasn't all of it. He said: "Tom is in there. You saw him go in, didn't you?"

Johnny laughed. "Do you see him comin' out?"

Lew looked at the house. It was still dark and quiet. Whatever was happening in there, it didn't show out on the street. All at once he thought of Rose. He thought she was still asleep inside. His panic exploded into a quality of fear he had never expected in himself. He turned and looked at Johnny. "You're going to leave Rose alone—"

"Shut up and get inside."

Johnny's voice, the set expression on his face, the way he carried himself—it all added up to something different. Something in Johnny Broom's pale eyes told Lew that he had gone somewhere far out beyond reach, into a darkness that passed his understanding.

He went up the brownstone steps.

The door stood ajar. Darkness waited beyond.

"Inside, Lew," Johnny said again.

He stepped through the old-fashioned tiled vestibule into the darkly shadowed living room.

He saw Rose first, on the floor near the couch where Flopsy still slept. He saw Mike, the other boy that Pete Broom had described, knowing instantly that this was the one who had been with Johnny at the warehouse. He saw Mike rise from Vallera's dark figure on the floor, rising like some thin, vicious beast of prey. He looked at Vallera incredulously. He couldn't believe that the tough old sergeant had gone down like that. For a moment he thought Vallera was dead. Then he saw the older man lift himself on his elbows and drag himself to the couch.

"Rose ..." Lew whispered.

"She's all right," Mike offered. He grinned and giggled. "Just sleeping it off." He had two guns, Lew saw. One was Tom's spare. Again Lew felt a wave of disbelief, a sensation that this couldn't be happening here in this house. He felt Johnny push him, and he stumbled forward, moving beyond where Vallera sat, breathing heavily, wiping blood from the side of his head. Lew dropped to his knees beside Rose.

"Rose?" he said wonderingly. "Rose?"

She breathed quickly, erratically. He saw the bruises on her face and on her body under her thin, torn dressing gown. He looked at Flopsy, not understanding the other girl's sleeping presence, and then he stared at Johnny. Johnny had pushed Mike aside and stood in front of Vallera's numb figure.

"How come you didn't kill him?" Johnny asked Mike quietly.

"I don't know," Mike said. He giggled again. "I sure tried. He's tough, like an old rooster."

Vallera said in a croaking, harsh voice, "You'll wish you had, boy, if I ever get up on my feet again."

"You won't," Johnny said. He cocked his head to one side. "You seen Stitch?" he asked Vallera.

"The Pollard boy? No."

"He's in the dining room. Dead. You killed him."

Vallera muttered, "I didn't know I nailed anybody. How did he get here?"

"We made him walk."

"You didn't get a doctor?" Vallera whispered hoarsely.

"No."

"So you punks just let him die," Vallera sighed.

Johnny looked as if he were going to bend down and hit Vallera to finish what Mike had started. Then he changed his mind. He turned and spoke in quiet command. His voice was different. He was in command now.

"Get some water," Johnny ordered. "I want Vallera on his feet. I want him cleaned up." Mike sensed the change in Johnny and nodded in obedience and started for the kitchen in the back of the house.

In the kitchen, he looked nervously at the clock on the yellow wall. It would soon be daylight. He ought to be thinking about getting out of this pretty soon now, to give himself enough time to get back downtown before it turned light. But he drew a saucepan of water at the kitchen sink and then picked up the long kitchen carving knife he had carried earlier and thrust it into his belt before returning to Johnny.

Lew had lifted Rose from the floor and was sitting with her on the couch, supporting her in the bend of his arm. Rose's head rested against Lew's blue-uniformed chest, and Lew was whispering to her quickly and urgently. Her eyes were closed, and now and then she gave a small, negative shake of her head, as if she denied and rejected his words.

Flopsy had awakened and stood, dazed, in a corner of the room, sucking her lower lip.

Johnny splashed the water unceremoniously over Vallera's battered head. He paid no attention to the others. Vallera coughed and dashed the water from his face and then pulled part of a slip-cover off one of the living room chairs and tried to clean the blood off his face. He started to rise and looked around. He stared at Lew and Rose, and then at Johnny.

"You want me on my feet, punk?" he whispered.

He tried to lunge up. Johnny laughed at the way the old man just wouldn't give up. He placed his foot against Vallera's thick chest and shoved hard, and Vallera crashed back against the piecrust table that Mike had daubed with paint. The table fell over and Vallera squatted, panting, still trying to clean the blood from his face.

"Stay cool, you bastard," Johnny said softly.

Lew said, "What do you think you're going to get out of doing this, Johnny?"

"A car. Some dough," Johnny said. He grinned. "A real clean getaway."

"You're out of your mind. You've done enough for tonight." Lew's voice was cold and flat. He was the only one who didn't seem to be afraid, since Vallera didn't count anymore. "Throw away your gun," Lew said, "and give it up."

"Don't sound me, man," Johnny said. "Don't needle me." He dangled the car keys in his left hand. "We're all going for a ride, you see. All of us. Everybody in the house. We'll go over to Camden and into Jersey."

"In the police car? They'll stop you at any of the bridges."

"You'll do the driving," Johnny said. "You'll say the right thing, or Rose gets it. You understand how it'll be? I'll have a gun at Rose's head, in the back seat."

"But Tom and I are due to be called down at the Hall any minute," Lew objected. "They'll notify us on the radio. We're supposed to be standing by for the D.A."

Johnny stared blankly at the young cop. "So what? So you just won't get there, is all."

"But if we don't answer the radio call, they'll come looking for us," Lew said urgently. "I'm telling you this because I don't want any gunfight with Rose in the car. Don't you see? Look, we all know what you did, Johnny." He took a deep breath. "There's no out for you except to give yourself up and pay for what happened tonight. Surrender and end it. End it right now, before something worse happens."

Johnny laughed. "What could be worse, man?"

Rose whispered suddenly: "Johnny, let me help my father. Please. He's been badly hurt."

"He's lucky to be alive," Johnny snapped. "Stay where you are."

He walked back and forth across the shadowed room. He felt high, as if he'd just had two or three sticks of pod. He was in control here. Whatever he said was the law. He'd learned things tonight that made sense at last. He knew what fear was, for himself, and he learned what fear of others toward you could mean too. And since leaving Pete, he knew that he was alone, really alone. The way they looked at him now, with their big, staring eyes, some of them dumb with fear, like Flopsy and Rose, others cold and quiet, like Lew—it just meant they were afraid of him, and they'd take whatever orders he cared to give.

He didn't like this business about the car being called down to the Hall. That complicated things. He knew that Lew was telling the truth. It made sense, and he grinned suddenly, thinking of what all the big shots must be doing right now, running around like chickens without their heads, because Henry Dexter Stephens was dead. All at once Johnny didn't regret anything, not one bit of what had happened. It was the way things were meant to go, he thought, and it was only the beginning of things, not the end. He would see to it that it wasn't the end. Nobody paid any attention to you unless you forced them to, made them look at you and respect you through fear and force.

"All right, so we'll change our plans," Johnny said confidently. "Flopsy, you go outside and sit in the car."

Flopsy started with surprise. She looked skinny and tired, Johnny thought. He was through with her and with girls like her. From now on, there'd be girls like Rose for him, real lookers, real class. He'd live high, all right.

"Whadda ya want me to do that for?" Flopsy whined.

"You just sit in the car and listen to the radio, hear?" Johnny swung back to Lew. "What are your call numbers?"

"Two-two-one," Lew said flatly.

"I told you not to sound me," Johnny warned. "Rose gets it first if you try any con tricks."

"I know that," Lew said grimly. "Those are the right call numbers."

"Good," Johnny said. "When you hear them, Flopsy, come in here fast and let me know. And stay down on the seat, out of sight, so nobody can see you. Anything goes wrong, blast the horn."

"I wanta go home," Flopsy whined. "I'm tired and I don't feel so good anymore—"

"You do what I say or I'll kill you," Johnny said quietly.

Flopsy went out quickly.

Johnny swung the gun to cover Rose and Lew and Vallera.

He bounced a little on his toes. In the gloomy

shadows of the room, he seemed taller than he had been before.

"Here's what we'll do," he said quietly. "If you get called down to the Hall, Lew, you and Vallera will just go down there and answer the D.A.'s questions like you said you'd have to."

"Are you crazy?" Mike burst out. "You can't let the cops go. You can't trust them!"

"Shut up," Johnny said. "I know what I'm doing."

"But they'll spill—"

"They won't say anything about us being here," Johnny said. "Because we'll have Rose with us. You understand that, Lew?"

"Yes," Lew whispered. "But the way you beat up on Tom, they'll ask questions about what happened to his face—"

"He can say he fell off a fence while he was chasing me up an alley," Johnny said, grinning. "And maybe, if the D.A. asks you to identify me, you won't be so sure about it anymore, huh?"

Lew didn't reply. He held Rose tightly to him.

Johnny laughed aloud. "I like this idea even better. When you're through down at the Hall, you both come back to the house. We'll all spend a nice, quiet Sunday in here, all of us together, get it? We'll let the heat cool until tomorrow night. Then you'll go rent a private car for us, Lew, and bring it around and we'll take off for a long, long ride. You were right, using the patrol car, that'd be a crazy idea. It was Mike's brainstorm, anyway. This idea of mine will work a lot better."

Mike licked his lips. "Suppose they bring more cops back instead, Johnny? You can't trust them, you know that."

"Lew knows better than to cross me. I'll kill Rose.

He knows I'll do it, because I've got nothing more to lose."

"Count me out of it," Mike decided. "I can't stay here all day tomorrow. I've got to get home."

"You'll stay," Johnny said decisively. "One of us will sleep while the other keeps things under control."

Mike's face was thin and dark with anger. "You don't understand, man. I didn't cut in for all that time."

"You cut in and you stay in," Johnny said harshly. He turned a little and his gun covered the dark-haired boy. "Toss your gun and Vallera's rod over on that chair. Do it easy, you know?"

Mike licked his dry lips again. "Don't point your gun at me, man."

"Then do as I say."

Mike saw the rigid hardness in Johnny's eyes, and he hesitated only a moment. Then he took one gun after the other and dropped them into the upholstered chair beside him.

All at once, when he looked around, he saw that the quality of the shadows in the room had changed. He could make out a dim grayness beyond the window.

Dawn was coming.

And panic began to lift in him.

Chapter Seventeen

Mike watched the light strengthen with increasing anxiety. On none of his previous expeditions into the Jungle had he stayed out so late, and he knew that with every passing moment his danger of being identified increased. During the night, the friendly shadows helped to conceal him. But soon the church bells would start their tolling, and Sunday would begin. People would appear on the streets, trolleys would run more often, there would be traffic everywhere. And down on Society Hill, the big clumbering house would stir and waken. If he were found to be missing—

This last idea of Johnny's was crazy, this staying holed up here in the cop's house. That wasn't the way Mike had planned it. He couldn't remain here all through the day. If he did, it could mean the end of everything.

His terror began to mount swiftly, compounding and feeding on itself. He stood silent, watching the two cops. Vallera was better now. He sat on the floor, breathing heavily like a wounded bull, his eyes glowering under his heavy brows. Mike wished he had killed the old man. He'd tried, but the old bastard was even tougher than he looked. He wished Vallera wouldn't keep studying him in the brightening light. He knew Vallera was trying to remember him, and he turned away a little, on the pretext of checking Flopsy outside in the patrol car. She was still there. He began to hope the call would come through for, the blues to go downtown. That would leave him alone with Johnny, and maybe he could reason with Johnny or do something to get out of here....

He knew that if he just tried to walk out now, Johnny would kill him. Johnny had changed since he went to see his brother. He seemed more sure of himself, and his certainty had added to his deadliness.

Now for the first time, he recognized the fact that this whole thing had gotten beyond his control.

He wished Vallera wouldn't keep staring at him.

He wished Flopsy would come in with the word that would take the two cops away.

He wished he could tackle Johnny—

And then he knew he had to. In self-defense. He couldn't stay here any longer. The windows were definitely gray now, and a thin breeze crept through into the room, touching his face with a feeling of dawn.

He still had the knife he had picked up in the kitchen. He felt the cool length of it against his side, tucked under his belt. Johnny hadn't noticed it.

Maybe he wouldn't need it.

"Johnny," he said. "You got a smoke on you?"

Johnny was standing just inside the entrance from the street door, looking out. "No."

"I think there's a pack of butts in the kitchen. You want one?" If he could get to the kitchen, Mike thought, he could just walk out of the back door and be gone before Johnny had any idea of it. He said, "I'll get 'em in a sec."

"Never mind," Johnny said.

"But I just—"

Johnny turned his narrow head and stared at him. His eyes looked hollow in his face. His voice was flat and the grin that carved his mouth didn't touch his eyes.

"Stay here where I can see you, Mike."

"What's the matter?" Mike protested with pretended indignation. "Don't you trust me?"

"No," Johnny said.

That was that, Mike thought. He hooked his thumb in his belt and his fingers touched the wooden haft of the kitchen knife there.

Vallera saw Mike touch the knife. He sat still, his thick shoulders braced against the wall, and tried to ignore the aching furious pain in his face where the boy had clobbered him. The beating had served one purpose, anyway. It had squeezed the alcohol out of him in one great gush of sweat, and he was cold sober now. Cold sober and thinking clearly for the first time in several hours. And angry with a different kind of anger from that which had possessed him before.

Animals, yes, that's what these boys were. He always said it, and he'd keep on saying it. They had renounced society and decency, and made outcasts of themselves, fitting themselves to a primitive gang code that consisted of rumbles, bopping, pod parties, the girls no more than adolescent prostitutes, their only rules being the ones they created for themselves.

So when a man dealt with animals, with dangerous beasts who rejected the laws of morality and civilization, the only way to win was to remain a man, to use your brains and your skill to cope with crazy emotion. That was where he had been mistaken before, Vallera thought. Outsmart them, move faster than they could, not try to outrun their young bodies, but use ambush tactics, surprise, and then, only then, the ultimate force of society.

Vallera breathed deeply and let the air out of his aching lungs in a long, silent sigh. Lew was right, too, in many ways. You couldn't whip these punks into line, because they had nothing to lose. You had to offer them something, like Henry Dexter Stephens had tried to do. Sure, Stephens was dead, and Johnny had gunned him down, but that wasn't the point of it. They were kids, they didn't know what the world was like, and it was up to the civilized ones, the adults, the ones with experience and the power, to show them how to live in the world today.

Vallera didn't know how to do it. He knew that somewhere in the past decade things had passed him by, changing, with new outlooks and new problems that evaded his grasp.

He looked sideways at Lew McGee, and he felt a

rupturing pain in his heart when he saw the way Rose leaned against McGee, the way she was hurt and clinging to McGee. He'd been lucky up until now, Vallera thought. Something like this could have happened long ago. If he had listened to Rose and moved out of this house, away from the neighborhood—

But that was wrong, too. You didn't solve things and answer problems by running away from them.

You stayed where you were and fought it out. So nobody was altogether right, and nobody ever altogether wrong, either.

He saw, with grudging respect, that Lew was behaving well for a young cop, just out of the rookie class. He kept his head. He didn't try anything foolish, as he himself had done, fighting against overwhelming odds. It wouldn't do any good to trigger these crazy kids into violence too soon. The violence would come of its own accord. He could feel it building up as the light grew stronger. This boy, Mike, was getting nervous. He wanted out. You couldn't talk to him, though, and work on his nerves to make him break. Johnny Broom was too smart to permit it. It had to come by itself, building up slowly. But it was coming, the violence. Vallera could smell it.

The thing to do when it came was to use it for yourself, to go with it and bend it and make it do what you wanted.

Make it finish things here.

That was the way you outsmarted a young animal who was faster and stronger than you, who wasn't inhibited by all the laws to which you, yourself, subscribed.

Take their strength and bend it so it worked for you.

Take their violence and turn it against themselves.

Vallera told himself to be patient. It was coming soon. He looked at Lew and Rose again and wondered if they knew it. He hoped Lew would do what he could to protect Rose when it happened. It wouldn't be long now, either. He heard church bells suddenly ringing over the streets and alleys of the neighborhood, and he saw the way Mike started and began to tremble and then touch the knife again.

Rose felt Lew's lips brush her hair. She seemed to be awakening from some horrible nightmare, climbing slowly and painfully out of that dark abyss into which the boy, Mike, had thrown her. She stirred and felt the strength of Lew's arms around her.

"Lew?" she whispered.

"It will be all right, honey," he said helplessly.

"I'm sorry ..."

"There's nothing to be sorry for."

She began to shiver and her teeth chattered and he held her tighter. "You don't know what they did—those boys are so strong—"

"Don't talk about it."

"Lew, do you love me?" she whispered.

"Always."

"Even though—?"

"Nothing happened," he said, and he kept the anguish buried somewhere deep inside him, throttling it and killing it, or else he knew he would go crazy. "Nothing happened at all, you hear?"

"I want to marry you, Lew," she whispered.

"We'll be married. There won't be any more waiting."

He saw Johnny grin at him from across the room. The light was stronger, brighter. A car went by on the street outside, tires whining as if the asphalt were wet.

It was the first sound of life he had heard from the world outside. He felt as if he had been imprisoned in this deranged, vandalized room for an eternity. But it hadn't been more than an hour. And it was going to end soon. He saw what Vallera saw, and he, too, waited and prayed....

Mike couldn't wait any longer. He was beginning to think the cops had conned Johnny with all that talk about expecting to be called downtown any moment. But Johnny believed it and Johnny was willing to wait. That was all right for Johnny; waiting didn't cost him anything. But time had run out for Mike, because morning had come.

It had to be now, before another minute went by. It would be bad enough, getting home at this hour, as it was.

He kept his thumb hooked in his belt and got up and crossed the room toward Johnny. The panic in him gave him a breathless feeling, different from the excitement he had enjoyed all through the hours of the night. He didn't like it; he told himself to stay cool. He made his voice quiet when he spoke to Johnny.

"Man, I've got to go. I just can't stay any longer."

Johnny looked bleakly at him. "You stay."

"I can't."

"You have to run home to your people before they find out you've been bopping tonight?"

"I don't want to bug out, Johnny. But it's like you say. You understand?"

"You cut yourself into this. Nobody invited you. But you just don't punk out on me. You don't go chicken, you hear?"

"It isn't that. But I've got to get home."

"Where is home?" Johnny asked. His eyes were

cruel. "Where do you live, Mike?"

"I—I can't tell you."

"I ask you, you've got to tell me, man. I'm holding a rod on you. Tell us all. Then you'll be in on it all the way with me, see? You've got a last name, and the cops want to hear it. So tell it, and then we travel together for good, you and me."

Mike understood now. If the cops learned his name, then there'd be no quick dash for home and safety, no lying in cool, clean sheets in his bedroom there, watching the light brighten on the pattern of his mother's colonial wallpaper print, no re-living the fun and the excitement over and over again, in the serene safety of home.

"I'm going," he whispered. "Now, Johnny."

"You won't go far," Johnny said.

He raised the gun. Mike saw that Johnny was going to shoot him. Johnny was beyond caring about any noise the gun might make. Nothing mattered to Johnny anymore. He was gone, out of this world, worse than if he was high on pod or horse. He didn't know or care about danger. He thought he could handle anything now. And Mike's flesh flinched and cringed, as if he could already feel the impact of Johnny's bullet in his belly.

The knife jumped into his hand and he drove it home.

Mike screamed something at the same time, and he knew he was screaming he couldn't stay, and all the time he pushed on the knife, feeling it go in and go deeper.

Everything seemed to come apart then.

Johnny's gun crashed and Mike felt the floor jump under his feet with the impact, as the heavy slug smashed into the carpet.

Vallera came up in a low, driving crouch and

slammed into Mike, spinning Johnny away with the knife in his belly. Johnny hit the wall head-first and stood there, gasping, bent forward, supporting himself with his head pushing hard against the solid wall. But for Johnny the wall wouldn't stay solid, it kept slipping away and melting, and there was this pain in his belly, a terrible anguish, hot and hard, something alien inside his body that had cut and eaten the life out of him....

He tried to get the gun up. His arm felt like water. He couldn't understand what was happening. He tried to deny the pain, but it was there, and a great wave of warm shivering came up through him. He turned his head sidewise, his cheek pressed hard against the cool wallpaper. Somebody was crying softly. It was Rose Vallera. He saw her sitting on the couch, and she stared at him and wept, her bruised face twisted with pity.

Hell, she didn't have to feel sorry for him, Johnny thought. What was she bawling for?

All at once he was sitting on the floor and he had his hand on the end of the knife that protruded from his stomach. He couldn't figure things out. He had been running all night, but he didn't know now whether he had been running toward something, or away from something. It didn't matter, anyway. He was too tired to run anymore. He had tumbled down all through the long, long hours, down those dark steps, and now he saw what had been waiting for him all this time at the very bottom.

He saw it clearly, with eyes that widened and stared, and didn't close again....

Pete Broom heard the shot distantly, while he lay in bed in the front room of the house diagonally across from Vallera's. He knew it wasn't a backfire.

He could tell the difference.

He felt something wrench inside him, and he stirred out of his exhaustion and sickness and got off the bed to look down at the street. He saw Vallera's patrol car parked in front of Vallera's house.

He saw a girl—Flopsy Gann—get out of the patrol car and run away, up the street and around the corner. Nobody followed her.

He knew the single shot had come from inside Vallera's house, and so he knew where Johnny had been hiding since he'd left here.

The crazy, shook up kid.

He wondered if there was anything he could do. Maybe he ought to go over there, anyway, even though he was sure it was too late to do anything. And in all the years past, since Johnny had been a baby, then a toddling boy, and Pete was left with the responsibility—in all those years, Pete hadn't known what to do for him, anyway. Nor did he know now.

He went back to bed and sat down gingerly, then stretched out on his back and stared at the ceiling and listened to the church bells ringing in Sunday morning.

Vallera tried his best, but there wasn't much left in him, after he got Johnny's gun away. He stumbled in Lew McGee's way and Lew tripped over him as he plunged toward the back of the house after Mike's darting figure. Lew never said anything about it afterward, when he returned from the kitchen.

"Are you all right?" Lew asked at first.

"Yeah. Yeah." Vallera breathed heavily and looked down at Johnny's pale blond head, at his strong, thin body curled on the floor, curved around the knife in him that Mike had put there. "He's dead. It's over."

"I'll call Precinct," Lew said.

"Take the gun," Vallera said. "I'm betting we can trace it to Comber. Comber must've given him the gun."

Lew said, "I thought Comber was your pigeon."

"Not anymore."

Vallera stood up. He felt tired. The night was over, and more than the night had ended. A great many things had finished for Tom Vallera tonight. He went over to Rose and touched her cheek. He felt clumsy about it, but she looked up at him and her mouth shook. He wanted her to smile, but she didn't.

Lew said, "Stitch Pollard is in the dining room, all right. Your bullet got him, Tom. They weren't lying."

"No." Vallera drew a deep breath. "I'm sorry about that. What about that Mike kid?"

Lew went over to Rose and made her stand up. He kissed her and held her tight. Today was Sunday, so nothing could be done about getting a license at the Hall today or about getting their physicals. But tomorrow would be all right. There wouldn't be any trouble with the D.A., now that they had Johnny Broom.

"Rose?" he whispered.

She shook her head and went to the window. He followed her and made her turn around and kissed her again.

"We'll get married right away," he said.

She looked at her father.

"Anything you want, honey," Vallera said. "Whatever you say, Rose. Lew will be fine." It was the first time the older cop had called Lew by his first name. He turned away and asked again: "What happened to that Mike boy, Lew?"

"He got away," Lew McGee said.

Chapter Eighteen

Mike returned home in broad daylight. He still found it hard to believe his luck in getting clean away, and it was still only a few minutes after six. It was a gray, cloudy Sunday, and the thunderstorms that had threatened all night had degenerated into a thin, warm rainfall that felt good on his head and shoulders as he walked up the driveway to the back of the big, safe, brick Georgian townhouse of the Tarrants.

Actually, he told himself, there was no reason to have been so panicky back there. Things always worked out for him. And they always would. Nobody would ever catch him.

And the night had been one to cap all the others put together. He had manipulated events very well, he thought, and he had acted with the objective courage of the superman, the god who made the clods of ordinary people dance to the tug of strings.

He felt better now. His fears were gone. He was safe, and the warm, steady rain that fell made him feel refreshed and sated, gorged to repletion with the night's events.

He entered the house silently by the back door, paused to listen for a moment. The big house was still asleep. He wondered if his parents knew yet about Henry Dexter Stephens. It would be fun listening to them talk about it today.

Lord, he was tired.

He hadn't realized how long and busy the night had been. Slowly, Mike bent and took off his shoes and went up the back service stairs in his stockinged feet. His clothes were a mess, and he had had to walk a good part of the way downtown, once he escaped from Vallera's place, rather than risk attracting attention on public transportation.

After tonight, of course, he would have to stay out of that particular section of the Jungle. That old bastard of a cop would be sure to recognize him, if they ever met again. But Mike knew that the chances of their paths ever crossing once more were one in a million. And in his usual clothes, in an outfit selected from the crowded closet of his bedroom, he wouldn't look the same, anyway.

He'd have to try the South Philadelphia area after this.

Or maybe he could organize his own bopping gang from some of the fellows right here on Society Hill. Most of them were soft punks, but there were a few who had that restless look that Mike knew so well. It was an exciting thought. He'd have to give it a lot of consideration—

"Michael?"

His whispered name stopped him in his tracks. His heart jumped and pounded erratically. Then he looked up through the dawn shadows in the silent stairwell and saw Jane Quarles leaning over the banister rail up there on the third floor. Her round moon face looked distorted by her anxiety.

He went on up to her.

"Michael, dear, just look at you—"

Her hands fluttered, patting him. He brushed past her and went into her room. "Is everybody asleep?"

"Yes, but your mother and the doctor came home *very* late." Jane closed the door softly and leaned back against it. She wore a ridiculous transparent pink nightdress that showed him clearly, and was designed to do so, all the fleshy, rounded, maternal curves and hollows of her soaped and scrubbed figure. "Mike, poor darling, you look just *awful!* Here, let me help you—"

"Take your goddam paws off me," he grumbled tiredly. He wondered if he had the energy to resist her, and then saw the placid, comfortable smile on her round face. "What's the matter?"

"You're bloody," she whispered. "Bloody all over!"

"Keep your voice down!" he snapped.

"Yes, sweetheart. But—were you hurt?"

"No."

"Please, Michael. Let me help you."

He sat down on her wide, rumpled bed, so full of precocious memories for him, and let her pull off his socks and dungarees. There were cigarettes on her night table and he helped himself to one. There was also the remainder of a bottle of Scotch and he twisted about to reach it, as much to evade her anxious, fluttering hands, touching him here and there. The liquor was good and smooth—his father's stock—and he drank greedily. It made him feel better.

He glowered at the tropical fish in Jane's stupid tank under the window.

"We heard about Mr. Stephens, Michael," Jane said softly.

He looked down at her bowed head, considering the thick strands of her braided hair. He knew what she wanted. He was sick of her; the thought of her disgusted him. "Yeah?"

"You don't seem surprised. You know about it? Such a terrible thing!"

"I heard."

She lifted her head and looked up at him with strangely level, bright eyes. "Where did you go tonight, darling? What were you doing all these terribly long hours while I waited here and worried so much about you?"

"Look, I've got to get back to my room," he said.

"Oh, but you promised—"

"It's morning, already."

"And it's raining," she pointed out. "They were up late." She referred to his parents. "They'll sleep late. We have hours, sweetie. All to ourselves. I waited so long for you, Michael."

"That's what you think." He stood up, his knee hitting the side of her head, pushing her aside. She didn't mind. She smiled up at him. He toed the rags she had taken off his body and didn't care, didn't think it mattered, the way she looked at his naked body. "I'm tired and I'm going to turn in."

"Michael," she whispered softly. "Were you there?"

"What?" he asked.

"Was it you? Was it?"

"What are you talking about?"

"The blood on your hands. And on your clothes. It's not yours, because you're not hurt. I don't care, I don't mind anything you do on nights like this, sweetest. You can tell me."

"There's nothing to tell," he muttered.

"You killed Mr. Stephens, didn't you?" she whispered. "Didn't you, Michael?"

"What if I did?"

"I told you, I don't care. I don't understand it, and I guess I don't want to—not as long as you always come back to me and let me take care of you like this, darling. I know how you are, and I know you can't help yourself. You need me, you know. And you should be kind to me."

"Jesus," Mike exploded. "Won't you ever stop?"

"Tell me, did you kill him?"

He thought of Johnny Broom, and the death of Johnny and the murder of Stephens blended and melted together in his mind. "Yeah," he said. "I was there and I helped."

She smiled.

She went to the door and locked it.

"You'll stay here with me, then, for a while," she said.

He felt quick anger. The liquor he had just drunk was warm and good inside him, giving him new strength to resist her. "What do you think you're doing? Don't play any funny games with me, Jane. I told you I'm not staying, and that's that. You make me sick, simpering and slobbering all over me. Like I was—like I was one of your goddam stupid guppies."

"Not guppies, Michael. All sorts, angel fish—"

"They make me sick!" he snapped. He wanted to yell at her, but he didn't dare. His anger and outrage at the way she behaved made him tremble. "You make me sick, too!"

"Michael—"

"Give me the key."

"No."

He swung away, thinking: *The stupid dumb bitch, she thinks she's got something on me. I ought to teach her a lesson....*

He looked at the fish tank and decided to do it. He was sick of Jane. And she knew too much, now. Tomorrow, he'd have to start figuring ways to get rid of her—

But right now—

Violence moved in him. He'd teach her a lesson. He couldn't touch her here, couldn't slap her or beat her, since it was too near the time when the house would stir and wake, and he couldn't risk the noise.

The fish, then.

She loved those stupid guppies.

He moved with the thought, crossing the room, turning away from her. He picked up the heavy, yellow-green tank with its festoons of ferns and dime-store mermaids and ceramic castles and carried it into the adjoining bathroom and, all in one movement, before Jane could stir or cry out, he dumped the whole mess, fish, ferns, water, ceramic gadgets and all, down the toilet.

Then he pressed the flushing lever and watched the stupid business go whirling round and round and vanish down the drain.

He walked back and put the empty aquarium tank down on the table under the window.

Jane hadn't moved.

She stared at him and wept in silence.

"Now give me the key," Mike said.

"Yes, dear."

Jane waited for twenty minutes after Michael was gone, standing still in a kind of numb agony.

Then she couldn't stand it anymore.

He was just a boy, and she was past thirty, and she had made an utter, total fool of herself with her helpless, hopeless, useless, sacrificing love for him.

Loneliness could make you see things and dream things in a blind, crazy, unreal way. And it could make you not see things that stared you straight in the face, things you ought to see and avoid.

She shivered and gasped and went over to the aquarium tank and picked up a shred of fern. It clung wetly to her finger. It trembled, as if it had a life of its own, but it only trembled in sympathy to the way Jane shook apart inside, facing the truth.

Looking into the empty fish tank, she saw Michael Tarrant very clearly.

He was sick, sick, she thought; he needed help.

She gave herself the full twenty minutes, and then she went down to the second floor and listened outside Michael's bedroom. He was asleep. She could not imagine the wicked dreams he must be dreaming.

Satisfied that Michael slept, Jane went downstairs to the telephone in the front hall and called the police.

THE END

Edward Sidney Aarons was born in Philadelphia, Pennsylvania in 1916. He attended Columbia University, working as a reporter, a salesman and a fisherman, and in 1933 winning a collegiate short story contest. He continued writing stories for such publications as *Detective Story Magazine* before publishing his first novel, *Death in a Lighthouse*, under the pseudonym "Edward Ronns," which he would use for most of his career. Aarons is best known for writing the "Assignment" series featuring CIA agent Sam Durell beginning in 1955. He wrote 42 "Assignment" books in all, selling more than 23 million copies in 17 different languages. He also sketched, sailed, did cabinet-making, was a camera enthusiast and a deep-sea fisherman. Aarons died of heart ailment in New Milford, Connecticut on June 16, 1975.

Edward S. Aarons Bibliography
(1916-1975)

Assignment series: Sam Durell
Assignment to Disaster (June 1955)
Assignment—Treason (April 1956)
Assignment—Suicide (November 1956)
Assignment—Stella Marni (April 1957)
Assignment—Budapest (October 1957)
Assignment—Angelina (March 1958)
Assignment—Madeleine (August 1958)
Assignment—Carlotta Cortez (January 1959)
Assignment—Helene (March 1959)
Assignment—Lili Lamaris (August 1959)
Assignment—Zoraya (March 1960)
Assignment—Mara Tirana (September 1960)
Assignment—Lowlands (January 1961)
Assignment—Burma Girl (January 1961)
Assignment—Ankara (September 1961)
Assignment—Karachi (September 1962)
Assignment—Manchurian Doll (1963)
Assignment—Sorrento Siren (January 1963)
Assignment—The Girl in the Gondola (March 1964)
Assignment—Sulu Sea (1964)
Assignment—The Cairo Dancers (1965)
Assignment—School for Spies (1966)
Assignment—Cong Hai Kill (1966)
Assignment—Palermo (1966)
Assignment—Black Viking (1967)
Assignment—Moon Girl (1968)
Assignment—Nuclear Nude (1968)
Assignment—Peking (1969)
Assignment—White Rajah (1970)
Assignment—Star Stealers (August 1970)
Assignment—Tokyo (February 1971)
Assignment—Golden Girl (September 1971)

Assignment—Bangkok (May 1972)
Assignment—Maltese Maiden (November 1972)
Assignment—Silver Scorpion (June 1973)
Assignment—Ceylon (November 1973)
Assignment—Amazon Queen (April 1974)
Assignment—Sumatra (October 1974)
Assignment—Quayle Question (May 1975)
Assignment—Black Gold (November 1975)
Assignment—Afghan Dragon (June 1976)
Assignment—Unicorn (1976)
[series continued as by Will B. Aarons, ghosted by
Lawrence Hall]

Non-series:
Nightmare (1948)
Escape to Love (1952)
Come Back, My Love (1953)
The Sinners (1953)
Girl on the Run (1954)
Hell to Eternity (1960)
The Defenders (1961)
Deadly Curves (2017)

As by Edward Ronns

Death in a Lighthouse (1938; reprinted as *The Cowl
of Doom*, 1946)
Murder Money (1938; reprinted as *$1,000,000 in
Corpses*, 1942)
The Corpse Hangs High (1939)
No Place to Live (1947; reprinted as *Lady, the Guy is
Dead*, 1950; reprinted under original title as by
Aarons)
Terror in the Town (1947; reprinted as by Aarons,
1964)
Gift of Death (1948; reprinted as by Aarons, 1970)

The Art Studio Murders (1950; reprinted as by
    Aarons, 1964)
Catspaw Ordeal (1950; reprinted as by Aarons, 1970)
Dark Memory (1950)
Million Dollar Murder (1950; reprinted as by Aarons,
    1973)
State Department Murders (1950; reprinted as by
    Aarons, 1965)
The Decoy (1951; reprinted as by Aarons, 1969)
I Can't Stop Running (1951; reprinted as by Aarons,
    1971)
Don't Cry, Beloved (1952; reprinted as by Aarons,
    1967)
Passage to Terror (1952; reprinted as by Aarons,
    1963)
Dark Destiny (1953; reprinted as by Aarons, 1973)
The Net (1953; reprinted as by Aarons, 1972)
Say It With Murder (1954; reprinted as by Aarons,
    1968)
They All Ran Away (1955; reprinted as by Aarons,
    1970)
Point of Peril (1956; reprinted as by Aarons, 1965)
Death is My Shadow (1957; reprinted as by Aarons,
    1965)
Pickup Alley (1957; movie tie-in)
Gang Rumble (1958)
The Lady Takes a Flyer (1958; movie tie-in)
The Big Bedroom (1959)
The Black Orchid (1959; movie tie-in)
But Not for Me (1959; movie tie-in)
The Glass Cage (1962)

As by Paul Ayres

Dead Heat (1950; based on radio series)

Black Gat Books

Black Gat Books is a new line of mass market paperbacks introduced in 2015 by Stark House Press. New titles appear every other month, featuring the best in crime fiction reprints. Each book is size to 4.25" x 7", just like they used to be, and priced at $9.99 (1–31) and $10.99 (32–). Collect them all.

1 Haven for the Damned
by Harry Whittington
978-1-933586-75-5

2 Eddie's World
by Charlie Stella
978-1-933586-76-2

3 Stranger at Home
by Leigh Brackett
writing as
George Sanders
978-1-933586-78-6

4 The Persian Cat
by John Flagg
978-1933586-90-8

5 Only the Wicked
by Gary Phillips
978-1-933586-93-9

6 Felony Tank
by Malcolm Braly
978-1-933586-91-5

7 The Girl on the Bestseller List
by Vin Packer
978-1-933586-98-4

8 She Got What She Wanted
by Orrie Hitt
978-1-944520-04-5

9 The Woman on the Roof
by Helen Nielsen
978-1-944520-13-7

10 Angel's Flight
by Lou Cameron
978-1-944520-18-2

11 The Affair of Lady Westcott's Lost Ruby /
The Case of the Unseen Assassin by Gary Lovisi
978-1-944520-22-9

12 The Last Notch
by Arnold Hano
978-1-944520-31-1

13 Never Say No to a Killer
by Clifton Adams
978-1-944520-36-6

14 The Men from the Boys
by Ed Lacy
978-1-944520-46-5

15 Frenzy of Evil
by Henry Kane
978-1-944520-53-3

16 You'll Get Yours
by William Ard
978-1-944520-54-0

17 End of the Line
by Dolores &
Bert Hitchens
978-1-9445205-7

18 Frantic
by Noël Calef
978-1-944520-66-3

19 The Hoods Take Over
by Ovid Demaris
978-1-944520-73-1

20 Madball
by Fredric Brown
978-1-944520-74-8

21 Stool Pigeon
by Louis Malley
978-1-944520-81-6

22 The Living End
by Frank Kane
978-1-944520-81-6

23 My Old Man's Badge
by Ferguson Findley
978-1-9445208-78-3

24 Tears Are For Angels
by Paul Connelly
978-1-944520-92-2

25 Two Names for Death
by E. P. Fenwick
978-195147301-3

26 Dead Wrong
by Lorenz Heller
978-1951473-03-7

27 Little Sister
by Robert Martin
978-1951473-07-5

28 Satan Takes the Helm
By Calvin Clements
978-1-951473-14-3

29 Cut Me In
by Jack Karney
978-1-951473-18-1

30 Hoodlums
by George Benet
978-1-951473-23-5

31 So Young, So Wicked
by Jonathan Craig
978-1-951473-30-3

32 Tears of Jessie Hewett
by Edna Sherry
978-1-951473-36-5

33 Repeat Performance
by William O'Farrell
978-1-951473-42-6

34 The Girl With No Place to Hide
by Marvin Albert
978-1-951473-49-5

35 Gang Rumble
By Edward Aarons
978-1-951473-53-2

Stark House Press
1315 H Street, Eureka, CA 95501 707-498-3135
griffinskye3@sbcglobal.net www.starkhousepress.com
Available from your local bookstore or direct from the publisher.

www.ingramcontent.com/pod-product-compliance
Lightning Source LLC
Chambersburg PA
CBHW070957190726
48292CB00004B/1490